PRAISE FOR **Paul Almond's**
The Deserter

"Can you talk about thrill-a-minute Canadian history? You can now. Paul Almond has worked for many years as a TV and film director, and his skill shows in the drama and pacing of this first-rate read." *Carole's BookTalk*

"I believe this one should be placed into the hands of every young student learning the history of Canada.... Paul Almond's portrayal of the Mik'maq is very accurate, he embraces the true circumstances and includes the significant legends of the people." *Mrs. Q Book Addict*

"Paul Almond...has created characters with great finesse. The readers will find themselves rooting for this likable and inspiring hero." *The Gaspé Spec*

"Readers will find this book an easy way to learn more about the English and French pioneers, and the Micmacs indigenous to the area, as they begin to create a new society incorporating all three." *Suite 101*

THE
SURVIVOR

Also by Paul Almond

The Deserter
Book One of the Alford Saga

THE
SURVIVOR

BOOK TWO of the ALFORD SAGA

PAUL ALMOND

McArthur & Company
Toronto

First published in 2011 by
McArthur & Company
322 King Street West, Suite 402
Toronto, Ontario M5V 1J2
www.mcarthur-co.com

Library and Archives Canada Cataloguing in Publication

Almond, Paul, 1931-
The survivor / Paul Almond.

(The Alford saga bk. 2)
ISBN 978-1-55278-967-4

I. Title. II. Series: Almond, Paul, 1931- . Alford
saga ; bk. 2.

PS8601.L56S87 2011   C813'.6   C2011-901330-4

 Canada Council   Conseil des Arts
for the Arts   du Canada

 ONTARIO ARTS COUNCIL
CONSEIL DES ARTS DE L'ONTARIO

The publisher would like to acknowledge the financial support of the
Government of Canada through the Canada Book Fund and the Canada
Council for our publishing activities. The publisher further wishes to
acknowledge the financial support of the Ontario Arts Council and
the OMDC for our publishing program.

Design and composition by Szol Design
Map design by Szol Design
Printed and bound in Canada by Webcom

10 9 8 7 6 5 4 3 2 1

For Joan

as always

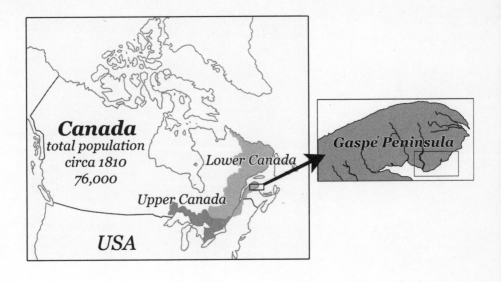

Canada
*total population
circa 1810
76,000*

Lower Canada

Upper Canada

USA

Gaspé Peninsula

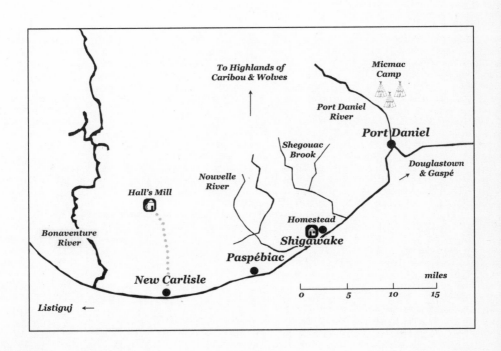

*To Highlands of
Caribou & Wolves*

*Micmac
Camp*

*Port Daniel
River*

*Shegouac
Brook*

Port Daniel

*Douglastown
& Gaspé*

*Nouvelle
River*

Hall's Mill

Homestead

Shigawake

*Bonaventure
River*

Paspébiac

New Carlisle

miles

0   5   10   15

Listiguj ←

Chapter One: 1813

Thomas Manning strode through the woods a couple of miles back from the bay, fighting a powerful despair swarming over him like the ever-present black flies. Baby son off with the tribe, well looked after but still, wife gone, and nothing, ever, could replace Little Birch. All spring, ever since he had left his Micmac encampment up the Port Daniel river, he'd fought this battle against melancholy. But now, something drove it from his mind.

The smell of smoke.

Could it be a forest fire? No, probably some settler on the move. But who'd travel inland, so far from any settlement? More likely a couple of the local Natives, passing through. Yes, having lunch. He dismissed the thought.

And then of course, relentlessly, the images haunting him for the last month took over: the first time he and Magwés, his wife, had revealed their love. He had been spending the winter back in the interior with her family, and she had called him out of their wigwam. He followed her on snowshoes to a nearby hill, and then she had said, "Thomas, look up."

He had never seen such a display. The spectacular curtain of light wavered across the Northern sky, streamers of red and purple shimmering in a filmy curtain, surely hung by some impressive Micmac deity to dazzle them both.

They stood as one, watching the light — dancing, it seemed, only for them.

In that clear, icy night, he looked down into her dark eyes, alight with the pleasure and reflection of the lights. His heart hammered as he heard her breathing grow deeper, quicker, as though she had been running.

Then, at the same moment, they leaned close.

Their lips met.

That rush of blood which flooded his lungs and his heart leapt in him again, as he walked the spring woods, and drove him to shake his head angrily, repelling the image. You're just torturing yourself, he complained, over and over again.

He walked on, looking for the patch of blueberries in a burned area well back by the brook. He also wanted to find cranberries left over from winter, or shoots of squawberries, bearberries, or wintergreen, all of which he'd eaten with the Micmac. But most of all, he wanted to get Magwés out of his mind. Focus on your search, he told himself.

The smell of smoke intruded once again, and he stopped to test the air. Yes indeed, there, to his right, much too close, a stack of black smoke!

Nothing in his walks as a lad over the Derbyshire countryside had ever prepared him for this. Two summers ago, while working for the Robin's Company in Paspébiac stogging a new hull with oakum, he had heard talk of these wildfires.

Ahead of him, an explosion of accumulated gas blasted the spike of a charred trunk that twisted into the air, fell, and more flames broke off to continue on the rampage.

A storm had passed in the night; the thunder had

woken him in his cabin and lightning had illuminated the bare interior, but this morning, the earth outside was hardly damp. The woods did need rain; this spring had been unusually dry. Travelling over a tinder of dead leaves and pine needles since dawn, Thomas had begged the Lord Above to bring rain.

He whirled and headed for the Coast. Living among the Micmac had taught him how best to navigate these woods. But as he glanced back, he saw the fire was gaining on him; soon he'd be caught. He should never have lost himself in a welter of morbid recollections.

He looked up. Flames raced from treetop to treetop with the speed of a catastrophe; the roar reverberated through the vast woods. He'd be burned alive.

Get going! his brain yelled. But where? All at once it hit him — the brook. Yes, down in the Hollow. But where was it from here? How close? Head back, quick, to the valley's lip. Dangerous. But how else to reach it?

Behind, the fire charged through the trees, pouring flames upwards. Smoke thickened and swirled, threatening to choke him. To his right, another spruce burst into flame. And another.

The land sloped up. Did that mean his direction was wrong? But beyond that, it might drop into the Hollow. He looked anxiously left and right — fire on both sides, galloping flames leaping from tree to tree, circling the trunks, savaging the tops, roaring as it tore at flammable needles and cones that swirled upward in buoyant plumes before falling to set other spot fires. Ahead, another tree caught fire.

Surrounded.

Think, check your choices. The brook was the only

alternative. He saw the tufts of trees surging with crimson fire, but below, yes — a way through. Should he risk it? Behind him, the blaze whipped up a whorl that flared into the sky. He'd stepped into an oven.

He dashed below the burning tops with flaming limbs dropping all around him. A branch struck him on his shoulder; he slapped the embers away. Ash in sudden up-drafts scattered down to blind him. He blundered through scratchy branches, leapt deadfalls, got clear — and there, beyond, the woods dropped away.

Frantic, he tore over the brow and down. Too steep. He tripped and fell, over and over, somersaulting, until he struck a tree trunk. Stunned, he tried to rise, the bloodthirsty fire chasing him, but he slumped back, ankle throbbing, shoulder wrenched.

He lay still for a moment. Get up! he commanded himself. Unsteadily, he rose to his feet and set off down-ward. But his ankle, twisted in his tumble, gave way. He resorted to pulling himself past trunks, his shoulder hurting. Finally he reached the bottom, humped with dead trunks, fallen limbs, dead moss, dry ferns. A brook did run somewhere here, he knew that. But how far? Its gurgling would be drowned out by the raging firestorm. Downdrafts hauled smoke around him, making him cough. Even down here he could feel the heat intensify. His heart hammered and his mind swirled like the fire.

Behind, the blaze raced along the brow of the hill. Any second, it might drop down to cut off his progress. Find that brook fast.

Knots of tangled bushes blocked his way. How could they flourish under these Balm of Gilead, themselves survivors of another fire? Their heavy foliage topside was being devoured. He forced himself through more snarls of shrubbery to join a stampede of mice and voles, even a fox.

Where was that wretched brook? He plunged into a thicket, but he'd lost his sense of direction. Was he actually going in a circle? His coughing intensified, draining his energy and slowing his pace. The smoke was settling down around him, stifling his breath.

Above the flaming trees, thick clouds still darkened. Promise of rain? He prayed aloud for a cloudburst. Save me, he begged, scraping past barbed branches of spruce.

Trees exploded, limbs splintered and snapped — taking him straight back to the gun deck of the *Bellerophon*, with its roar of cannon and cracks of musketry as Naval Marines picked off sailors on their battle-ravaged decks. Once more he recalled exhorting his gun crew, fighting back the panic that immobilized lesser men. Keep cool, the unspoken motto of every sailor in His Majesty's Navy. In the extremes of battle, think clearly, do your duty. He remembered Lord Nelson's signal, fluttering from the distant *Victory*, translated by their Signal Middie astern: "England expects every man to do his duty." How his gunnery mates had resented that! With the great Battle of Trafalgar approaching, what else would they do? What else had they been doing? Treat us like men, they clamoured under their breath, wheeling out their giant cannons in readiness: what else would we do but our duty?

So he made himself keep cool now, plunging toward the hoped-for brook. Still the explosions reminded him of the great 32s on his gun deck, as a pine beside him exploded. A gust of oxygen had struck another build up of gasses — and boom, the tree showered Thomas with flaming debris.

Race for the brook. But which way? He glanced upward as flames attacked more Balm of Gilead, and suddenly he found no surface for his feet.

Down he crashed, into the brook. At last. But too shallow. Shocked by the icy water, stunned from striking the brook stones, he tried to lift himself but fell back into the running water. He choked, then shook off his confusion, rose shakily onto all fours. No! First roll over and soak your clothes, and then your long hair.

Quickly, he struggled up. Find a deeper pool. He ran on, his feet slipping on mossy stones, and tripping. He pulled his shirt up over his head. The brook turned. Was it still too shallow? After another fall, he pulled himself out onto the bank and lurched forward. Among the crack of dry branches resembling musketry, he thought he heard shouts, as if from his men, exhorting him: "Go Thomas, save yourself, we're with you." His crew, his gunners...

And "go" he went, leaping branches, dodging more deadfalls with the fire chasing him. Then he saw a grizzled birch, aslant. Yes! he'd fished there — that was the pool.

A limb fell just in front of him. He stopped. It ignited a thicket of dead brush. He dove back toward the brook. Just keep your footing, he prayed, slipping and slithering up the stream-bed toward his pool.

A muskrat scuttled straight back into the fire. No, he shouted, wrong way! He stooped to save it. Panicked, it whirled and raced past. He straightened and kept going.

His back burned, his feet and ankles pained, but he dropped once again into the icy brook, dousing his six-foot frame, lean from two years surviving in the New World, burying his long hair and beard which was already drying rapidly. The bushes around the brook caught fire.

Now what? His flesh seared; he choked from the smoke: it tasted bitter and acrid. He dropped onto all fours, keeping close to the water. For some reason, the lower air let him breathe. His elbows and knees scraped on the rocky bottom.

A blackened trunk athwart the brook stopped him. He tried squeezing beneath it. Some bark came loose and he grabbed it, forced himself under and past the ring of fire, splashed the last ten feet and then collapsed into the pool.

On his back, completely submerged, he lifted his face to breathe. Too hot. He placed the bark over his face to shield him from the heat. But his fingers burned. Was the fire passing over? All at once, he couldn't breathe. No oxygen. Suffocating.

He tried gulping air. Calm down, he told himself, slow that beating heart. But he couldn't. He felt he was drowning. With a huge effort, he made himself resist the urge to leap up and gasp for air. Better suffocate in this icy water than die by burning. Torn by impossible choices, his mind flashed with visions of a Native woman. Magwés, Little Birch, his wife, dead and gone these last two months. She reached out her hand. Her touch calmed him as he felt himself fading. And then as her vision drifted away, the fire seemed to pass over.

A breath of air filled his lungs. The intense heat was lessening. Soon he lifted out his face, then his body.

The fire had thundered on, passing over him in its wild rampage, and he heard the sound of thunder. More lightning? No, he reassured himself, just rain. Rain at last.

Chapter Two

A couple of days later, Thomas sat on the stoop of his cabin in the Hollow and marvelled at how the providential rain had rescued him as he lay freezing in the brook. Whittling a spoon, he now tried to sort out his dilemma. Freed for a while from his haunting despair, the fire had shocked him back into reality. Again he offered thanks to the Lord Above.

Now take stock of the situation! Decide whether to stay, or to leave to find a job. Two summers ago, he had worked with an old British master-caulker on a Robin's Company barque, the workhorse sailing vessel that Robin's often used. Being on the run from the Navy at the time, it had offered a convenient disguise, but hardly enough money to accumulate all the tools and a draft animal needed for the farm he hoped to start. He had not accepted M'sieur Huard's offer of work last summer; instead, this spring he had brought Magwés back to his cabin and worked at clearing his land for their life ahead. He quickly put that darkening thought out of his mind.

Perhaps he should travel east along the Coast to the tiny settlement of Pabos. That was probably a couple of days paddling, and so manageable. But he'd not heard of any employment there. About a hundred miles further on at the mouth of Chaleur Bay lay Douglastown, another English settlement. But that was out of the question.

Too far away to paddle, expert though he had become.

He could stay here, plant a few potatoes and some maize, the Indian corn, or possibly cabbages, but he was sure that would not keep him alive through the winter ahead. He could fish through the ice, trap small game — he knew how, after that one winter with the Micmac. He could live alone, slowly clear his land, cut trees, saw them into lengths with the fine tools M'sieur Blanquart had given him, after Blanquart's son Marc went back to France to look for Sorrel, the little sister.

He wondered how the old man was doing. He had enjoyed his son Marc's companionship in the woods last winter among the French lumberjacks. Again he'd seen how you needed neighbours here in the New World. One man alone could not survive. You needed the interconnecting relationships of friends. His cabin was far from any such community, nor would any spring up soon, given that winters were severe and the land only brought forth bounty after back-breaking work, guaranteed to make even the stoutest of hearts quail.

So that, in a way, decided him. Working here with no friends, no companionship, and of course no possibility of finding a wife to share his life as Magwés had done, would not further his cause. During these last two years in the New World, crammed with life-threatening episodes and all the challenges of an uninhabited terrain, he had learned one thing — you made things happen yourself, or you lost out. So for better or worse, he had better get out, get to Paspébiac, and try his luck.

Having decided, he leapt up, and spent the rest of the day preparing his camp for the leaving thereof. He hid his few tools in a cache he'd dug a hundred yards upstream from his cabin. Then he climbed out of the Hollow and on out toward the bay, to look down on the site of his proposed farmhouse. Below this hill, flat land ran down to the red cliffs overlooking the sea.

Not much to show for all his work, with about twenty feet or so cleared. Giant trunks lay awry, limbed and gaunt, awaiting oxen to drag them to the walls he hoped to erect over foundation stones lugged up from the beach. Among the stumps he'd planted some potatoes and corn from the Micmac. Yes, it would look like any abandoned site of a would-be settler, and passersby were unlikely, anyway, his place being miles from Paspébiac. Travellers up and down the Coast used only the sea: no land transportation through thick, impassable forest and rivers to be forded.

He and Magwés, Little Birch, had mapped out this place for their eventual farmhouse, chosen because this hill would cut the north wind, and the flat land would accept a farmhouse, a garden, and buildings for livestock. This is where they had intended to stay until the end of their days. And now, her days had already ended, so abruptly.

He paused, and bowed his head, trying to keep tears from starting into his eyes. But start they did. His son would be well looked after by the Micmac band, he knew that, much as he longed to have him with him. But, of course, quite impossible. He waited for a while, then cleared his throat, and got up and walked down to the brook, where he got himself a good long drink of water, and then returned to his cabin to prepare for his next foray into the unknown.

***

The next morning, Thomas Manning sat in the stern of his new Micmac canoe, paddling with strong, even strokes past the high, red, ragged cliffs strewn with birds. He marvelled at how these helldivers wrung a satisfactory living out of their sparse environment, when he could not yet make a go of it by his lush brook. The spring had produced for him some wild onion root, very young leaves of willow that were nice and tender, and of course the one week's produce of fiddleheads. But he had no more molasses for energy, flour for bread, and most important, no salt for curing, nothing in fact of the many supplies on which life depended.

He hoped this canoe trip might free him from his loneliness but no, his isolation remained. He had loved Magwés with all his heart, and it seemed so very cruel that she had been taken from him by the birth of his only son, now looked after by the tribe.

Above, reaching out like some mournful ghost, a floating cloud with dark undersides had taken over the pale sky. The weather here in the Gaspé was so changeable. An east wind meant rain. But right now, the wind had let up briefly. The stillness might indeed presage a storm.

He paddled faster. The shoulder wrenched in his fall during the fire still troubled. His ankle throbbed too, though kneeling in this position helped avoid some of the pain. But as the rough weather approached, his natural confidence began to evaporate.

He loved the feel of the paddle, its white, polished birch handle fitting nicely into his palm. The blade was shaped like a willow leaf, pointed, unlike the settlers' rounded paddles. He tried to breathe deeply as he drove on, to summon up his ever-present good humour. His canoe had been a godsend. What a surprise he had felt when that Native delegation arrived at his brook! Wending down the cliffside, he'd seen the Chief among them.

Nothing had been said during the appropriate welcoming ceremony back at his cabin, the smoking of the pipe, the exchange of news, while his curiosity had built. Finally, the Chief revealed they had come to present him with a special gift: this fine canoe and paddle. The humped-back design featured an elevated gunwale (raised sides that curved upward in the middle, and also at each end) to provide stability in rough water, as well as being navigable in both shallow streams and the ocean. Several of the tribe's best craftsmen had fashioned it to demonstrate their appreciation for Thomas having risked his life to save that of their Chief. That fateful day he had gone, as a deserter, back to his man o'war, the *Bellerophon*, anchored off Paspébiac. With the invalided Chief in his canoe, he had paddled toward certain punishment, the one thousand lashes ending in death. But he put the memory aside.

On the cliffs, the cormorants wheeled and squawked their raucous objections to his passing, while ungainly squabs flopped about on the beach where they had landed after a first flight. Great gulls, some with black backs, others lighter grey with predators' faces, all circled to voice their strenuous objections to this intrusion. He nodded to himself. Still and all, fine companions; nothing wrong with these birds. Just like you, I don't like being interrupted; I too want to be left alone. Not many of us passing — which meant, he realized, no rescue should he get into trouble. One or two rowboats might pass each month, settlers going east to Pabos, a good long journey. Otherwise nothing but the odd Micmac paddler, and these never disturbed the birds. After all, the Micmac had been here for centuries.

He gazed again at the brazen red cliffs, secure in their severe majesty. He wondered how long they had looked out across this immutable bay. How long had they stared at Micmac canoes, passing them down through the ages? What must they think of our tall square-rigged ships now plying the waters? What must they think of the cannonades loosed by privateers at those merchant ships they were about to plunder? Though not much of that now, with the 1812–14 war between the British and Americans coming to a close. What have we wrought, wondered Thomas, with the march of our so-called civilization? Were they any happier before we came, these great, red guardian cliffs of the vast forests behind?

If only we had left them alone to stare out over the vacant waters, self-sufficient, with only their Micmac inhabitants who neither ravished each other nor the land itself, leaving the great trees to flourish upward untouched. The Micmac took from among the forest sentinels only what they needed for their own survival. Nor did they trap and kill beaver for hats in London and the great capitals of Europe. They left the wildlife bounty to interact and accumulate. They left the moose and caribou to battle for survival with the wolf packs, where the fittest could benefit from the testing, and go on to reproduce braver and more supple offspring.

We need the rain, he decided, forcefully bringing his mind back to the present: let the tempest come, I'll get to Paspébiac. But that was just bravado. Gaspé storms were unpredictable in their ferocity, unmanageable in their scope.

To take his mind from the mounting wind and the increasingly rough seas, he looked ahead. Why, he asked himself, had he waited so long to make this trip? Because he knew there would be so little chance of success?

Perhaps his old caulking master would be hard at work on another barque. But he had turned down their offer of work last winter in the woods: M'sieur Huard, the company steward, would surely hold this against him. A tough negotiator, he paid so little, hardly enough to barter for needed supplies. And Thomas had to get food, and tools.

Smack! A wave struck the canoe and splashed over him. He glanced back. The waters of the bay, usually so blue, had turned an ominous black under the gathering clouds; white caps stood out vividly. He wondered how much further he had to go. More than an hour certainly. The wind, in its Gaspésian and wayward way, had begun to shift. Head out into the bay, he told himself, the waves were striking the canoe broadside. He paddled into them, focussing on seamanship. Better get a move on. That squall was building.

Sudden spray drenched him and nearly swamped the canoe. He turned in, heading for the shore. No, too rocky. But no time to dawdle. He bent low and stepped up his paddling, keeping the rhythmic motion learned from his native friends. Then, an errant wave almost flooded him.

He put down the paddle and grabbed the wooden bucket to bail fast. But another wave struck, all but capsizing him.

Don't bail; just drive forward. If only that cockamamy wind would not swing back.

But swing it did. For some reason, it seemed now to be coming off shore, swooping down over the cliffs and pushing him further out to sea. He paddled furiously, determined not to let the sea become his master.

When the wind let up, he shipped his paddle and tried again. After two quick bails, his canoe turned sideways again. He grabbed the paddle and with adrenaline pumping, stroked for dear life. First the fire, and now this — too much in just a few days. But then, he had spent weeks when nothing had happened, when he had just chopped and limbed trunks, piled brush with flies buzzing and ever-present loneliness keeping him company. Approaching disasters made one focus. And focus he did.

He tried bailing, and then grabbed his paddle. This became a rhythm: paddle paddle paddle, scoop scoop. But the sea, a worthy opponent, kept building waves; the wind swivelled and poured it on. Thomas against the elements, and the sea was gaining the upper hand.

Splash by splash, wave by wave, more seawater filled the canoe. If only he had a better bailer. His biggest saucepan, made of iron, would have been too heavy. Deal with what you have, he remonstrated, keeping the rhythm. But as he neared the shore, the gale struck in full force, and the rain bucketed down. Now the canoe would really sink.

He bailed furiously. The rain plastered his long hair, soaked his peasant jacket and ran between his shoulders and down his chest. He could not see the shore. His shoulders ached. His bent knees hurt. His hands froze, making any grip on the paddle hard. A blanket of fatigue covered him. Ridiculous! So close to Paspébiac — but even closer to Davy Jones's locker.

Waterlogged, the canoe would not respond and developed its own will. It bucked, rollicked, and dove, going its own foolhardy way. He tried hard to right it. Don't you fight me, he commanded; we're in this together. If you sink, I sink.

For a moment, it seemed to succumb to the waves. He bailed hard, scooping frantically. Load lightened, his worthy craft stayed afloat. He dropped the bailer, grabbed the paddle and with new energy, drove forward toward the beach.

Beach? Rocks only, he now saw. He'd smash the canoe on them for sure. Try and get round the point. No use; the sea drove him in. So he swivelled, tried heading out, only to be almost capsized by a huge breaker. Could he leap out? Too far from the shore.

Head in anyway. But those sharp rocks risked his precious canoe. No more trips to Paspébiac. No trips anywhere. But what could he do?

The rain stung his eyes, making it even harder to see. And see he must, if he were to navigate between the great red boulders that had tumbled from towering cliffs. Back-paddle fast, he told himself. Wipe your eyes. Try to see through the driving rain. Look for any opening that might admit your canoe. Meanwhile, he swivelled from side to side, righting the canoe, straining into the rain, praying the canoe would not fill up.

Then he saw an opening. With a last thrust, he drove the canoe forward. It leapt through the waves, rode a breaker fast forward into jagged rocks.

Get out and grab the canoe! A huge wave lifted him, held him poised to dash onto pointed crags. He swung the front, he lurched left, finally leapt out, good! Only waist deep. Flung by waves he grabbed the canoe, hauled it with him, fell under, surfaced, coughing and sputtering, grabbed again and yes, felt sand under his feet, pushed the canoe ahead. That opening, yes! Wedge it there, clamber out. Craggy rocks scraped his shins. He yelled in pain, slipping and sliding, and heaved himself up onto the rocks, yes, he'd made it.

He tried with freezing hands to grapple the canoe up, haul it close, his hands hurt, his legs ached, but at last, he somehow got the canoe up too, and fell panting on the flat red rock. Would the storm last all night? How long could he survive in this icy rain?

Chapter Three

Freezing and shivering, Thomas curled under the tiny canoe at the base of the towering cliffs, wondering how he'd survive.

In the cold wind, he was reminded of the hapless Alexander Selkirk, whose story of a marooned seaman everyone on the *Bellerophon* knew, though not many had read the book. Back in England at Raby Castle, the noble children's tutor had lent Thomas *Robinson Crusoe*. Now cowering like a wet muskrat, paralyzed by icy spray and blasting rain, Thomas felt that, unlike Selkirk, he might not last the night.

Why had he left years ago to join the Navy? And his caring mother? She must be still working at the castle as undercook, her once lovely body worn down by years of unending toil. How he missed her! She remained in his mind, a spectre to comfort him. He resolved yet again to fulfill this obligation to write often, as soon as he got through the storm safely and had found a job. Somehow, the thoughts of Raby Castle, of his straw bed over the stable with the other lads, his regulated duties there, helped his brain to relax and, with all its chilled shaking, his body gave itself up to the fatigue that tugged him off into another world.

Two winters ago, when he had fallen through the ice, only the age-old wisdom and practices of his Micmac family had saved his life. And handed him an important lesson: when you start to freeze, keep alert, keep moving at all costs. He made a determined effort to uncoil his numb body and roll out from under his canoe. He got up into the blasting wind and began to move his arms, beat his frozen body, lift his knees.

What an endless night! So why not plan for the morrow?

First, go to the Paspébiac general store he had visited two years ago with his Micmac friends. But how to make himself presentable? No, his first steps should be the Robin's Company and Monsieur Huard.

Charles Robin had come from the Jersey Isles sixty years earlier, even before the fall of Quebec, and established a profitable cod-fishing enterprise. Through good management and hard work, the indomitable old fellow more or less controlled Paspébiac. He shipped cod by the schooner-load to Africa, Portugal, Europe, and finally England. Most families in Paspébiac were serfs of the Robin's Company, trading their summer's labour for the supplies sold in Robin's stores — a system known as the "truck" system. Thomas had worked for Monsieur Huard, the operations manager, and had even met James Robin, the nephew who now supervised everything, though important decisions were still referred back to Jersey Island where the Robin family originated.

So that must be his first effort, though he held out no great hopes. How he longed for the dawn; the night seemed endless as he pondered his bleak future, his spirit bound by chains of fatigue and despair.

Before dawn, the rain let up. The tide had dropped. Move your joints, he ordered, fight that numbness, lift down the canoe, get it onto the beach. So he muscled his canoe down onto the sandy area that had appeared in the night. He clambered back up to fetch his sopping belongings down into the upright canoe. Wading into the icy waves, he leapt into the stern and paddled hard. Paspébiac lay ahead.

***

An early glow from the east spread upwards, flushing away night and its horrors. The weather began to behave, promising a day of lustre. The light wind started to dry his clothes. Above, bodies of clouds relaxed in their blue watery heaven, stretched out like lazy swimmers on their backs, floating on homemade rafts, light and deft and airy. As he paddled on, the sun came up and beamed millions of sparkles of shimmering silver, a teeming carpet spreading across the dense, almost matted flecks of bay, westward toward a dull blue-grey and finally a misty blue at a southern horizon obscured by a morning mist. The rays seeped into his chilled body and flung wavelets of sparkles at his eyes. The surface looked as solid as pewter, as if you could walk across it.

He shipped his paddle and leaned forward to undo his belongings. One by one he wrung them out and stretched them on the thwarts of the boat for the playful sun to make up for the weather's horrible tricks of the previous night. He coaxed the canoe along with leisurely strokes to dry the clothes and warm his soul.

Around the distant point, he saw the Paspébiac sand-bank on which sat the buildings of Charles Robin, wooden warehouses, two, three, and even four stories high.

He scanned the waters for any sign of a British warship. Had His Majesty's Navy been so efficient as to spread the word of his reprieve? He still had to be cautious.

No Navy ships. The war between Britain and the United States ending meant fewer privateers in the bay, and hence fewer ships of the line coming across to protect these shipping lanes. After a time he paddled out around the sandbank, checking carefully before heading in for the dock. No point in hiding his canoe at the Micmac landing place, he headed straight for the heart of the Robin's operation on the *banc*, the large triangular sandbank, where he'd go to confront Monsieur Huard.

As he neared the floating dock, he remembered rowing out with his sick Chief to beg the surgeon of the *Bellerophon* to perform the operation that eventually saved the Chief's life. Since Thomas had deserted two years previously, his nemesis Jonas Wickett had been replaced. After Thomas had been captured by the marines and placed in the man o'war's brig, with no hope of escape from the thousand lashes, he had heard the heavy door clank open.

The Captain had entered alone, with word of the successful operation on the Chief. He went on to reveal that the Marquis, whom Thomas knew from his many visits to Raby Castle, had himself sent the Captain a very fine reward for having let his "ward" "escape" to the New World. Thomas had been taken aback by the largesse, with no idea why the nobleman had been concerned.

The Captain had interrupted his thoughts by saying, "So now I suggest you move rather quickly."

"Move, sir? Quickly?" Escape? He's letting me escape? Thomas could hardly believe his luck.

The Captain had leaned forward. "Go ashore a free man. But please, do take care to keep out of sight of His Majesty's Royal Marines!" He shook the hand of his former Midshipman, now still in shock. "I am sure you will continue to lead a full and righteous life here in the New World. Good luck and God speed."

A reprieve? But one thing Thomas knew for sure, he had to stay out of sight of the Navy for the time being.

He pulled in, tied up his canoe, and set off across the *banc* to the administration office. Two years before, he had trodden the same path, a fugitive from British justice, a deserter. Now, though he no longer had that stigma, he found his nervousness mounting. He so badly needed work. He strode across the same stoop and entered.

Seated at his desk, M. Huard lifted his head. *"Bonjour, young Thomas!"*

"Bonjour Monsieur Huard." Thomas bowed and removed his hat, pleased to be remembered. *"Est-ce que tout va bien avec la grande compagnie de Robin?"*

"Pas mal, pas mal, merci. And you, you're fine? *Qu'est-ce que tu fais ces jours-ci?"*

"Me? Oh, er, I have just escaped a big forest fire."

"Ah oui, ah oui, j'ai entendu, behind the *Canton de* Hope."

"No sir," Thomas began, then stopped — he didn't want to give away the actual location of his building site, so he played along. "I mean yes, yes, behind Hope. But it didn't last long."

M. Huard agreed. *"Oui. Mais ça prends du monde.* Much trouble. Many workers I send. I stop all work here two days. All the men, they thank the Lord for the rain.

They can achieve nothing without His help." He turned back to his books.

"Fires, they do seem beyond our control," Thomas agreed.

M. Huard was clearly busy, and Thomas was unsure how best to bring up the subject of his employ. "So," M. Huard asked finally, "what you come for? Work?"

"Yes sir." Thomas twisted his hat in his hand.

"Uh! *Malhereusement,* we have no place. We do not start the new ship before the next month. No caulking. Maybe in two months, we do some. Maybe come back then."

"But that's... August, the summer will be gone," Thomas blurted out.

"Ah oui. Mais c'est comme ça."

It's like that for sure, Thomas could see. He looked down. No work... He lifted his eyes. "But Monsieur Huard, I can learn another trade. You know I work hard."

M. Huard shook his head. "The boss, he say, dat's it. We have enough."

"Oh." Thomas nodded, but his heart sank. "Thank you, M. Huard. Thank you very much." He sighed for a moment before turning. He noticed a pained look flick across the supervisor's face before he returned to his books on the pine table.

Heading back to his canoe, Thomas found any optimism, any sense of good cheer, deserting him. What now? No food, no supplies, no tools. Another long paddle back to the lonely cabin? Those familiar black flies of despair returned in full force with this disastrous news.

Chapter Four

Thomas Manning sat on a bollard on the dock, and folded his arms. Time for a think. No job, no hope, and nowhere to go; things did look dark.

He couldn't leave his canoe here all day, now could he? He looked around. Gleaming white codfish lay under the Gaspé sun in long rows drying on their "flakes," or elevated flats of interlaced twigs. The fishermen's wives had turned them early this morning, once the rain had stopped and the dew dried. Across the sandbank, French workmen strode purposefully from building to building, carting bags of flour in wheelbarrows or leading oxcarts down the dirt road from the village proper. Everyone demonstrated a clear sense of purpose. Unlikely they'd steal his canoe, although it stood out as being unique. The French locals (including men from the British possessions of Guernsey and Jersey) were friendly to the Indians. The Micmac had helped defend the French and their settlements on Cape Breton Island, and then harassed the British after the French Acadians had departed south for Louisiana, the other French possession at the time, which the United States had purchased from Napoleon in 1803. So no, he felt the canoe would be safe.

But what should he do next? Who could he turn to? All at once it came to him. He'd worked in the woods two winters ago with Marc Blanquart who had then left in spring to search for his sister, Sorrel, in France. She had been abused by the master of the household where she had served. Had Marc found her? And what about Monsieur Blanquart, the father, how was he bearing up? Last summer he had appeared to Thomas much the worse for wear, hearing of his daughter's dire news from the slums of Lille.

Thomas soon found his way to the door of the Blanquart cabin by the edge of the woods, and knocked. The old man came out, and after a moment grabbed Thomas and hugged him as only a Frenchman would. Then he put kindling onto his open fire, and scooped up a kettleful from a rain barrel outside.

With a cup of steaming tea in hand, Thomas leaned back against the rough bark of the cabin to hear the news. Marc had indeed found Sorrel but in less than savoury circumstances.

M. Blanquart went on to relate how James Robin, not known for overwhelming generosity, had nonetheless offered Sorrel a passage, provided that on arrival she work as a domestic in his household. The child born from her master in France had been left in charge of a convent, and now she had arrived and was making a new life for herself.

"Tu vas la rencontrer ce soir" — You're going to meet her tonight, the old man told him. "You'll stay with us, oh yes, oh yes, no backing out." Thomas demurred but was overruled. And why not? Stay and collect his thoughts.

M. Blanquart gestured to the rough bunks with straw mattresses, one above the other. He would make a third in the opposite corner for Thomas.

"But what about Marc?"

Marc had no longer wanted to return to this harsh life. He had found work in the Old Country and would send money over when he'd saved enough.

That evening, after supping on a watery stew, Thomas took the dishes outside to help M'sieur Blanquart wash up.

"Regardes! Ma fille."

Thomas looked up to see a slim figure with a stylish gait coming down the trail. The girl stopped in her tracks.

Who was this strange man, she must be asking herself.

"Sorrel, Sorrel, viens!" the old man called. *"Mon ami est icitte. Il est venu nous voir."* My friend is here. He came to see us. *"Viens t'en!"*

In the moonlight Sorrel paused, shook her head, turned to go.

"Please," Thomas called, *"s'il vous plâit, mademoiselle,"* and continued in French: "Your brother has told me about you. We worked together in the woods, for Robin's. It was his wish that we meet."

She paused, undecided.

"She have hard time in France," the old man said. "No like men."

No wonder she hates men, he thought to himself as she came slowly forward. She was no doubt one of the more beautiful creatures walking the woods of the New World. Such large brown eyes, and waves of brown hair which had now begun to fall in wisps around her fragile face. Clear skin, a small nose uncommon among the other French here, she was a real eye-opener. But she'd certainly take time to become a friend.

Of all the inappropriate images that sprang to his mind, Magwés appeared, and oddly enough seemed to smile at him. He tried to rid his mind of the image, fearing it would throw him into black despair again, but no, it would not go.

The old man set to heating the remains of their stew. Sorrel had eaten at the Robins', but having worked into the evening, she admitted that she would like a bite, were it readily available.

Coming across on a Robin's ship, she had picked up some English from the other passengers, so she and Thomas were able to begin a broken conversation. He just could not take his eyes off her. As she sat sipping her soup, he observed her fingers, already roughening from the weeks in domestic service here. The way she held her spoon and her delicate gestures: all marks of table manners she must have picked up in the household of the French master to whom she had been sold. Her slight shoulders betokened a fragile frame, perpetually hunched as though in fear of beating. How he wanted to touch her, to reassure her, to help her truly relax.

Little by little, Sorrel did relax, unwinding enough to question him. Where did he live? How did he live? Under the enormous power of her two large eyes, Thomas found his own reticence disappearing. He rambled on about his cabin, careful not to reveal its whereabouts; he told her about the new site for his prospective farmhouse; he told her about his brook and the refreshment it would bring to any farm animals he managed to acquire, and even, yes why not, inspired by her, a puppy.

He told her how his brook wound down out of the dark hills of the interior. Yes, he did consider it now as his property. And then how his brook widened at its mouth to fall in great, red shelves of rock into the bay. He told her of his compartment in the hillside where he'd buried his tools, of his birchbark roof, and of his cedar bed built of saplings strapped together. They talked until her eyes drooped, and indeed, so caught up he had been in her presence that he had ignored his own drowsiness.

M. Blanquart had long since retired and now was breathing heavily on his top bunk. By common consent, they retired, but not before she had leaned over and kissed him on the cheek.

That set his mind churning. What indeed were those sorry circumstances in which Marc must have found her? Thomas guessed only too easily: she must have sold her body on the street, and probably for so little. He dismissed the thought. It means nothing, absolutely nothing, he said to himself. We all fall on hard times, and we all do what we can to survive. With the exhausting trip and his fight to survive on a shelf of rock the night before, he fell quickly asleep.

*　*　*

Thomas awoke to find the sun already high. He had slept long and felt deeply refreshed. But opening his eyes to such unfamiliar surroundings, he wondered where he was. An empty cabin? He lay back thinking. He retraced his footsteps, beginning with the night under the canoe, and then, the meeting with M. Huard, and finding no work hereabouts — ah yes, Marc's father, and Sorrel! He sat bolt upright. Where was everybody?

He listened. No sound, save for a far-off saw, and in

another direction, someone chopping wood. And of course, the perennial village dogs. He relaxed. The silence reminded him of his own cabin. But something was missing. The brook, the gurgling, that always kept him company. He got up, stretched, and then his eyes went to the workbench by a window he had not absorbed the night before. On shelves above it, half-carved shapes of tiny ships sat among odds and ends of small twine for the rigging, and pieces of roots shaped into small animals and birds. But where were all the tools? Only two — admittedly sharp — knives, to do all this? None of the chisels and fine instruments he'd seen in the carpenter's shop on board ship, nor in the cabinet-maker's on shore. A real artist, M. Blanquart, he decided. In his old age, too. So much the better.

But then, how much would he make from selling these trinkets to the odd sailors or visitors, or indeed any of the craftsmen who worked for Robin's? None of the latter would have money to spare, working under the "truck" system. Which reminded him of his own plight: such a tough world out there; without salt, he'd cure very little meat for the winter. Without wheat for bread, without the molasses or sugar to preserve berries, he'd never make it through. The more he thought about it, the further the lovely Sorrel receded, and the more desperate his plight appeared.

After helping himself to some breakfast from the food cupboard, he went outside to gather his things spread out to dry on bushes around the cabin. As he bundled them up to take back to his canoe, a vision of Sorrel flooded him with unconscious desires. Did that mean he was now open to having another wife? A momentary diversion, perhaps, but she had led him to realize that if he were to attract any young lady's attention beyond the first sprigs of conversation, he would certainly need something more tangible to offer than delightful descriptions of hopes and a few paltry dreams of survival. He would have to become a man of substance. A lot of work lay between these present doleful circumstances and his rather grandiose expectations.

The poor old fellow had obviously gone down to stand at the dock, or some village corner, to try to raise money for their evening meal. Meanwhile, behind the cabin stood a jumble of logs for the fire. Had Sorrel made enough, or perhaps bartered her summer's work, to acquire this fuel from the lumbering crews? He decided he had better cut and split some as a thank you for the old man, who so readily had given of his mite.

As he chopped and sawed, he pondered his next step. He would look over the town today, checking for any possible work outside the Robin's Company, though he knew little hope lay in that direction. And then what?

He remembered his visit to New Carlisle two years ago, when he had met William Garrett Sr., former officer in His Majesty's Militia and now a fine farmer. He had been given land, like many Carlislers, under a grant to all citizens who, after the American Revolutionary War, chose to head north and remain under British protection. These families were collectively known as United Empire Loyalists. Most of them had come north from what had been the Thirteen Colonies and now made up settlements here and in Douglastown, and many more in Upper Canada.

So off to New Carlisle he would go: seek first William

Garrett and his advice, even if it meant making contact with his three sons who had attempted to turn him in as a deserter, though admittedly when drunk. Would they not still want to gain the reward offered to tempt communities to turn in deserters? Might he not still be charged and thus incur a fatal punishment? A risk he had to run; he saw no other way. And of course, the thought of seeing the youthful Catherine again, after their fleeting moment together, was the incentive that moved him to action.

Chapter Five

Thrusting ahead through the choppy waters of Chaleur Bay, Thomas Manning tried to plan whom to see and what kind of work he might apply for. What about working on William Garrett's farm? No hope – his sons were quite sufficient for that task. What about another farm? There'd be a blacksmith, surely, perhaps two. And carpenters. He could take up a new craft. And he remembered the sawmills nearby. But with it all, he knew in his heart that money was in short supply hereabouts, and no one would really want to hire an apprentice.

He might have to go miles further up the Coast as far as Bonaventure, another French settlement. The *Bellerophon* had once anchored in off the village, which appeared to be as big as New Carlisle. But the crew had told stories of how, during the French–English war, the settlers had begun burning down their town to keep it from the British. They were not likely to welcome him, a sailor from His Majesty's fleet. No matter, with autumn and winter ahead, he had no choice but to find work.

His canoe gave him great mobility. How wise had been the Chief who had organized its making and giving. So should he return to the Micmac band? No, he needed money to become a full-fledged farmer landowner and farmer, his only goal.

Rounded billows of cumulus hung above the blue bay,

and above them, a thin stratum of mackerel clouds spread out motionless. Mid-grey gulls wheeled past, and further out a flight of gannets sped low in formation over the waters, heading toward Gaspé. On board ship, he'd passed their breeding grounds on an island off Percé, a hamlet with its curious offshore rock shaped somewhat like the prow of a ship with two holes in it. Someday, he would explore the rest of what he now thought of as "his" coastline. What a fine land! How rich in possibilities! The slap of the waves, the sweep of the paddle over the blue endless bay lulled him into a false sense of security. Indeed, what in the Old Country could ever match this? There, the sky was often so uniformly grey, laden with rain, and any rearing thunderclouds were swathed in mist. He placed his paddle athwart the bow and felt among his belongings for the last of his smoked trout. His water gourd had been filled at M. Blanquart's rain barrel. He ate quietly and drank his rainwater, first offering plentiful thanks to His Maker above.

Here he was, chewing on smoked trout, far from land, no ship visible, only himself alone with the gulls, and in the depths below, more riches than could ever be harvested: herring and mackerel, and along the bottom, flounders, mussels, and codfish. All his for the taking, if he worked long and hard.

He spotted New Carlisle on a rise ahead, above a point of meadows, and began to grow nervous. No doubt that warrant for his arrest lay still hidden in the files of the Justice Department. One slip-up might give him away, and before the Admiralty could be contacted, he'd be punished mercilessly. And what if his reprieve had been an *ad hoc* affair, brought on by the kindly Captain, but not really sanctioned by London?

Well, nothing he could do now but be very careful, and of course, change his name. He certainly sported a different appearance: his tousled sun-blonded hair and rough beard being so different from the well-groomed clean-shaven Midshipman who swam ashore one stormy dawn two and a half years ago. And he remembered grasping for another name to use that summer he had visited the Garretts. He should assume that. James, yes, that was the name he had chosen then on the spur of the moment, it being the King under whom his Bible had been translated. And Allmen, or Oldham, perhaps even Alford he had chosen. Yes, that's the name he decided he must use here in this haven of British loyalty. James Alford. Why not? He must remember that. Even though all his instincts told him to say, Thomas Manning, at your service. Now it would be James Alford, delighted to make your acquaintance, or some such polite rubbish.

When he had plunged off the good ship *Bellerophon* after all those years in His Majesty's Service, surviving war, disease, rats, and boredom — that too was a jump taken on the spur of the moment. But that escape had been long wished for. From then on, he could not attribute his finding the Shegouac brook to luck alone. He must first of all acknowledge the guidance of His Maker. He lifted his eyes to the skies, noticing at the same time the clouds building, and offered up a good dose of his daily quota of thanks: for his survival, for this wonderful beginning, for his magnificent (though by no means anything more than humble) home here in the uncharted wilderness of the Gaspé Coast. And especially, that start on a permanent farmhouse he one day hoped to complete.

He reached the dock, and moored his canoe. Beyond the sloping public lands, dotted with cattle and a few sheep like the commons of the Old Country, rose the village of New Carlisle. No church graced the cluster of homes, but these villagers had certainly found a way to make a fine living. Would they want to share it?

He climbed the dirt road and strode down one of the streets. The town was laid out on a grid, which had not caught his attention before on the short visit two years ago when he had come to post a letter to his mother and had thereby met the Garretts and spent the night. In Paspébiac, he knew the grid was based upon the seigneurial system, so the lots were narrower and stretched further back, whereas here the grid was square, perhaps because the English had settled here. He also noticed on the road back, two more houses being built. A good sign. People are more and more making a go of it, he thought with satisfaction, in spite of the grumblings and complainings the Loyalists were known for. A fractious lot, as his French co-workers had asserted.

He heard the sound of hammer against metal, and paused. A blacksmith! Perhaps he needed a helper? He turned northward up the dirt road toward the sound. He passed several smaller houses, simple squares with high, peaked roofs to shed the heavy snows, four windows in front, one on each side of the centre door and two on the second floor for bedrooms. Every house was whitewashed and had red ochre trim under black roofs with tarred shingles. Few had verandas, though further on he passed a couple with simple platforms across the front.

On one, he saw an elderly lady rocking and knitting, and waved. She smiled and called out a greeting. "Fine weather."

"The best," he replied, and kept going. Good idea if he did apprentice to a blacksmith: he might learn something of the trade that might be almost a necessity at his brook, being so isolated. Why not, indeed, set up a small forge to make the nails he needed, hinges for doors, latches, any number of items so necessary for a new home? Yes, he'd love that; his pace quickened and soon he turned in at an unpainted structure in front of a neat house.

The interior, darkened by years of smoke, was illuminated by the glowing fire spitting sparks as a huge red-haired smith pumped vigorously at his homemade bellows.

The newly named James doffed his hat. "Good morning, sir."

The smith grunted a reply.

"Fine shop you have here."

Another grunt signified agreement.

James leaned against one of the four posts used for a horse being shod. "Tap-tap-tap, dong-dong," sang the smith's hammer as he beat a thin, flat iron into a rosette-shaped piece, expertly punching holes in the glowing metal with small *hardies,* devices made to fit precisely into the holes of the anvil.

The smith chucked the metal into a half-barrel of water, and the sizzling gave rise to bubbles and smoke. He straightened. "What can I de fer ye?" he asked in a strong Scots accent.

"Well sir," James replied, "I wondered if you might need a bright young assistant?"

The smith eyed him. "I'm nae a money-bags, laddie, I'm a smith!"

"Oh no, sir. Of that I am well aware. But perhaps another body might increase your output, or avoid you turning down those many offers." James Alford smiled.

The smith replied by hauling out a large red handkerchief and blowing a resounding toot. "I have in mind some able-bodied man, but until I get all these offers ye speak of, I cannae afford one."

James wiped his brow with his sleeve. "Well, sir, that sounds like you might want an apprentice — someone who would work for nothing."

"Does it now?" He grinned and with his heavy pincers selected another piece of iron to begin another rosette, probably for a doorpost. James had noticed such decoration in front of the better appointed houses. Tap-tap-tap, dong-dong, went the hammer once again. "I might indeed."

"Well sir," James allowed, "'tis an offer to be thought over, for sure. If you would be good enough to hold it open for a day or two."

The smith's ample mouth broke into a kind of grin. "Not too many laddies hereabouts fool enough to sweat for nothing."

"But," countered James, "I presume 'nothing' would include a good midday meal?"

The hammer paused in mid-action as the smith looked across at him. He placed the sheet on the anvil and neatly hammered off a portion, and thrust it into the glowing charcoal and pumped the bellows. "Aye, I might be able to offer that, if ye're nae agin a big bowl of porridge with molasses, even a bit of milk from time to time."

"Better and better," James responded, and replaced his hat. "Well sir, my name is —" He stopped. "James," he said. "James Alford." Why not? Must get a start on this new identity, he realized, coming here now among British settlers. James paused in the doorway. "And you are, sir?"

The smith snorted. "Everyone knows me, laddie. There's only two of us, and I'm the better. Robbie Mac-Gregor."

"Why thank you, Mr. MacGregor. You'll be hearing from me."

"We'll see to that," said MacGregor. "We'll surely see to that." But then as James was going out, he called after him. "Och, listen, will ye, I've got a thing I'd pay for, if ye were of a mind..."

"Oh yes?"

"Charcoal. Most of it comes from the Old Country. Expensive. But the making, nothing to it. Ye could have a go at preparing me some. I'd pay ye fer that."

"Not considered the best nor cleanest occupation," James blurted out, not giving it a lot of thought, and partly to challenge the smith.

"No, but not the most difficult neither. Ye must only select suitable quantities of wood, build them into a bee-hive-like structure," the smith waved his hot tongs, gesturing, "maybe the size of a small house, make sure it's got some ventilation holes built in — the ends can be open or closed — and ye put over the top some sod or earth and ye start a little fire." He grinned, revealing large and somewhat decayed teeth. "Ye make it burn for, like, a month. Ye gotta control it, mind, so's it burns enough, but not too much, and doesn't burn up. Ye'd enjoy that, maybe?"

"I'll think about it, Mr. MacGregor. Thank you."

But as James passed down into the street, he said to himself: No sir! Not on your life! But otherwise, a start. Any possibility is better than none, he thought, as he started down a street toward the Garretts.

What next? He turned eastward toward another house with a shed in front that he remembered seeing on his previous visit. A simple sign outside proclaimed: John Gilchrist, cabinet-maker. He wondered if perhaps the cabinet-maker would be willing to part with a few pence a day for an energetic assistant.

James entered the yard where, in front of a shed, Mr. Gilchrist and his apprentice were making a long pine table. He's got one helper, James thought to himself, I doubt he'll need two. But no harm in trying.

So the conversation with the blacksmith was repeated once more, except this time to even less effect. One apprentice was all the cabinet-maker could handle or pay for. James gave his thanks and left.

Well, the moment had come to risk facing Will Garrett Sr. whose son Will had tried to turn him over to a JP in a drunken moment. But take time now, he thought, take in your surroundings. Should danger strike, better know the layout of the town.

A man passed him and doffed his hat. "Good afternoon to you, sir," he called, to which James replied, "Fine day."

"For sure, fine day 'tis."

Must be upwards of sixty dwelling here, thought James, a goodly settlement. Now multiply that by the number of wives, children, and their grandparents. Well established too. He knew the majority had come in 1784, almost seven years after the Revolutionary War, though many had left after the first few harsh winters to return to the Old Country or to set up homes in a slightly more temperate clime down in Nova Scotia. But here, these hardy remnants had clearly found a living to their liking. Walking along, lost in thought, he was overtaken by a girl who passed hurriedly.

Although she was dressed in a nondescript blouse and a billowing skirt, something familiar about her form made him hurry to catch up. Who was she? Blonde hair pushed up inside a pretty cap — yes! "Catherine!"

She stopped and turned. He saw by her colouring that she was stricken with astonishment. "You came back!"

How could he have forgotten that fraught night? He had been given shelter by her worthy parents, and offered padding next to the Garretts' dying fire, on that one and only visit. Something had made him open his eyes, and he had become aware of a singular presence enfolding him as he lay. He looked up and by candlelight saw her face, very close to his, closer in fact than any young lady had ever been.

"Ssh," Catherine had murmured, finger to lips.

She had leaned in close, so close he felt the feather touch of her light hair as her cheek brushed his, sending tingles down his spine. "I heard my brothers talking. Laughing and joking. Long into the night. At the general store, there's a notice about Navy deserters. They've decided you could be one of them."

James had tried to absorb it all.

She leaned in, looking deeply into his eyes. "You have to go, I fear."

Befuddled, James began to gather himself. But she hadn't moved. Their two faces, poised, began to merge.

He reached out and pulled her close. For one exquisite moment, their lips met. It seemed to him that her whole life went into this touch; for one delicious instant he felt his being joining with hers.

She broke away, flustered, and went to unbar the door. He gathered his coat and his pouch and hurried out.

Had it not been for Catherine's quick thinking, he might now be under the grass in the New Carlisle cemetery. The memory of her late-night kiss set his cheek burning once again. He had said then that he would return, a promise he was now keeping.

"Oh yes," he said, "did I not make a promise?"

"Two years is hardly keeping a promise."

James winced. "But Catherine, now that I remember, was it not you who made the promise?"

She blushed and dropped her eyes. "I... don't remember." She walked on and he quickly fell in beside her.

"So what are you doing here?" she asked.

"Coming to see you, of course. Why else would I venture into this den of iniquity?"

"What rubbish," she joked, with a slight edge.

"Yes," he murmured, "rubbish... of course."

They walked on for a few moments, in silence. She was even prettier than two years ago, slimmer, having shed some of her baby fat. Surely, even a match for the lovely Sorrel. Lovely complexion, no doubt, and such a sturdy body.

"And what makes you so hasty?"

"I had brought two dozen eggs to sell," she held out the empty basket, "and now I am hurrying home to help Mama with her supper."

There was a pause as they hurried on.

"Pray won't you join us," she invited at last. "I'm sure

my mother and father would be only too pleased to see you again." But there was something in her tone that James could not quite fathom.

"By all means, thank you," he replied brightly. "I have thought for a long time of your splendid family with great affection, and have anxiously awaited this return."

"Not so anxiously as to return in good time," she replied tartly.

Now how could he answer that? Something was amiss. What should he make of "in good time"? "I was hard at work constructing my meagre dwelling and trying to clear land for an eventual farm."

"Good for you," she countered, less than effusively.

He wondered what would happen when her brothers gathered from their fields for the evening meal. "How are your brothers?" he asked, in a roundabout way of reminding her of their adolescent treachery.

"Working very hard now," she replied. "You know, they were properly chastened by my father for their inexcusable lapse of manners when you were here."

"Lapse of manners?" They nearly had me killed, he thought to himself. But he didn't want to pursue that.

"Well, I am sure, all is forgotten now. They will welcome you as is right and proper. We are all of us duty bound to provide a welcome for any travelling settler."

The term "settler" pleased him. Yes indeed, he was truly a settler, though he hadn't yet thought of himself as such. But still, she sounded distant. "Oh I see," he said, "you think of me as just any old settler who must be accorded the welcome laid down by good manners?"

She glanced at him out of the corner of her eye, and let that fall unanswered.

"And how is your little sister, Eleanor?"

"Oh, you won't believe how she has grown!"

"I'm sure she has." James turned to study her as they walked on. What a lovely, healthy illustration of a working wife and future mother.

"But truly," she asked, "what does bring you to New Carlisle?"

"Work," he said, "I must find work."

She gestured ahead. "That's our house."

"How could I forget it?" They went up the steps, crossed the veranda, and entered another unknown.

Chapter Six

Eleanor Garrett, a tall, rather thin-faced woman with penetrating black eyes and dark greying hair in a bun, was putting a meal on the table, serving from iron cauldrons hung over the open fireplace. Catherine set about helping her with little Eleanor, about ten, sparkling eyes, happy as a kitten, putting big slices of bread into a basket — woven, James was quick to notice, by the Micmac. He could hardly take his eyes from the steaming mound of potatoes, carrots, and turnips that was to be their meal. How hungry he was!

Will and John entered, and James hastened to greet them, to demonstrate all had been forgotten. John, now eighteen, was inordinately handsome as well as personable, with black hair, dark eyes, and the kind of jaw one saw on statues. Will stood a shade taller than John, lean, almost ascetic, with a flat mouth and thin eyes from squinting in the hard winter sun. His long face gave him the air of a scholar, though he was hardly that: bold rather, almost uncouth. The two brothers could not be more unlike. The youngest, Joseph, about fourteen, was already at the table.

John gripped James's hand warmly. In contrast, Will Jr. appeared distant, throwing glances all the while at his sister, who was studiously ignoring them. Did that mean he took himself to be her self-appointed guardian?

"James!" John said as he put out his hand. "Good to see you again!"

"Good indeed," Catherine snorted, "since you both nearly had him killed two years ago."

"Oh, I'm sure he's forgiven and forgotten, haven't you, James?" John washed his hands under the indoor pump with a bar of homemade soap, and then dried them on the towel.

"Of course I have, John, no harm done." James quickly realized that he now must fully adopt this new persona of 'James', the name he had used previously. He turned to Will Jr. "And how are the crops coming?"

"Fair enough," replied Will curtly, the only one of the three brothers to have a hint of his father's North Country accent.

After pleasantries exchanged and much information traded, James brought up the reason for his return, the job hunt. Well aware that on the Garrett farm, the three brothers would be quite sufficient, he added, "Perhaps there might be another farmer, bereft of children, who might like a hand, sir?"

"A ton of 'em," William chuckled with the thick North Country brogue James loved, "but none as could pay anything." He clumped across from his chair by the window and took his seat at the head of the table. James had heard on his previous visit about William's leg wound received fighting in the Revolutionary War with His Majesty's Militia some thirty years previously. "Ye'd better not look to farming. Ye say ye tried that rogue MacGregor? I warrant he wants t'git ye for nothing." William sported a belly and a bluff manner common to the tough northerners of Great Britain. His grey hair was cut short, his hands large, the hands of a farmer. "And that John Gilchrist came here on the *Brig Polly* with me, he did. He'd never part with his money for another helper. He's got sons enough."

"That's about it, sir," James said.

"Now listen, there's not a lot of paying work anywhere on the Coast, once you pass up that rogue Charles Robin."

"But," James began hesitantly, as Mrs. Garrett placed heaping plates down for her sons, "New Carlisle seems a thriving community. Surely there must be some openings..."

William shook his head, and hammered out a brief grace: "God bless the lot of us and this fine table of food, and keep us mindful of Your presence in all things we do. Amen."

The others repeated Amen, and tucked in.

"What about the sawmill?" Mrs. Garrett finally sat down at the opposite end of the rough table, closer to the fire.

"What about it?" William growled.

"We do have a part interest in it."

"Sawmill's working just fine, luv. We don't want to interfere with old Hall and the way he runs it, now do we?"

Be bold, thought James: nothing ventured, nothing gained. "But perhaps, sir, someone eager and hard working such as myself might help him expand his operation. I'm not afraid of long hours, neither."

William threw him a hard look, but said nothing. James noticed Will Jr.'s eyes went to his father, but he too kept silent. What was going on?

Catherine seemed about to speak, and then said nothing.

John lifted his head, mouth full of vegetables. "He can try, surely Father, can't he? Might do old Hall a lot of good, to have a dynamic Britisher there. The others are all French." He grinned at James.

"That's all he can find," William mumbled sourly.

"It's back in the woods a good ways," Will ventured, and then looked at his mother. "Very out of the way."

Mrs. Garrett caught his look and paused, as William Sr. nodded absently, and mumbled, "Aye, might be better than nothing."

"Could you not write him a letter on behalf of our young guest?" Mrs. Garrett wiped her mouth with a napkin.

"We mustn't meddle, mind. Old Hall's been clear on that one."

"But dear, it's so out of the way..." She glanced meaningfully at Catherine. "And Mr. Alford might not mind living that far out from New Carlisle." William frowned, apparently trying to decipher his wife's devious mind.

"It's not meddling, Father." Catherine spoke up at last. "It's just giving Mr. Hall notice. Enlightening him on prospective employees. Surely we owe James that, after our family nearly had him flogged to death. If he wanted to go off tonight to take the letter... I could show him the trail, after dinner."

"I doubt anyone should go up that dreadful path after dark."

James looked up. "I'm not afraid of the dark, Mrs. Garrett. In fact, I rather like it."

"Pretty dangerous these days, James," the elder Garrett added. "Good many villains hereabouts. They think nothing of preying on poor passersby. Have to be careful, I'm sorry to say."

"Aye, no telling what's happened to New Carlisle these days," John offered. "Lots of lawlessness about."

"It's perfectly safe in the village," Catherine said. "I'll just show him the entrance to the trail. It's not so easy to find."

"Now Catherine, what would Billy say to that?" her father demanded.

"It's none of Billy's business," she retorted, colouring.

"I'd say it's all his business, now that you two are betrothed."

James lifted his head. What? Betrothed? Could that be true?

Catherine cast down her eyes as Eleanor spoke up. "Yes, isn't it exciting? Only last week William went off to meet Mr. Brotherton, and they concluded a nice arrangement. The Brothertons, you know, are one of the better families in New Carlisle. He's a Justice of the Peace, with large holdings." She paused. "It would be so nice for both of us."

"Well," James said in a calm voice, summoning every reserve of self-restraint. "I do hope you will be very happy, Catherine."

But for some reason, he felt as if the bottom had dropped out of his world.

**

Here he was, heading into the unknown again. But there was still plenty of light this late in the evening to see his way, being not long after the summer solstice. The track to the mill was scarcely large enough for a horse and cart, James thought, difficult for a team with a heavy load.

However did they get the lumber over this rutted track between these thick trees? And then how did they get the sawn boards back down?

After the Garretts' warnings, James began to be nervous. These sturdy two- and three-foot trunks appeared larger than in his Hollow: above, their interlocking branches blocked out the low sun, making the roadway ahead somewhat menacing. He kept his ears tuned, but all he could hear was the occasional crow, or moose bird, that would startle him with a scream as it swooped past. His practised eye picked out disused tracks, and former pathways of smaller game. The cart tracks were not fresh either. He knew the workers slept at the mill, so there'd be few passersby. Truly, he was here alone and undefended.

Too bad that in this land of plenty, some wretches resorted to banditry, a role assigned to highwaymen back in the Old Country. He remained on guard, but he'd left his flintlock back at the cabin, and carried only his knife in the Micmac pouch around his neck. How much good would that be?

As it grew darker, he began to doubt the wisdom of this expedition, every sense alert. And before too long, he heard the whine of the saw in the distance. He quickened his pace. Coming around a bend he saw the low, grey, hunched building, its weathered form somehow inviting. The river had narrowed at this point for the mill dam to reach across. The sluiceway ran with swift water, turning the paddle wheel. Two men, with long handled pick-poles, or pikes, actually walked on floating logs. He marvelled at their agility — not for him, he knew. Mr. Hall was certainly squeezing every last drop out of the daylight. Hard to make a go of it in these tough times, with little money changing hands.

He leaned against the rough boards of the building and watched the saw sing its way through log after log. Neat stacks of pale yellow boards lay beside an ever-growing pile of sawdust at one edge of the woods. The throb of the pulleys beat in his ears, a sound he decided he liked. It would slow its beat as the saw bit into a heavy log and then speed up again after it sliced off a board.

He went to look under the mill. Beneath the uneven flooring, a lad, an urchin really, wheelbarrowed sawdust onto a pile spreading into the trees. He seemed no older than little Eleanor, or perhaps just skinny so that he only looked young. After dumping the load, he turned to see James, and waved cheerfully.

James wandered over and the lad stuck out his hand. "Hello mister," he said. "I'm Ben."

"And I'm James, my lad. Are you the son of Mr. Hall?"

That did seem unlikely, with those ragged trousers and skimpy shirt, and more especially, a swarthy skin that could perhaps have only been darkened by the sun. But an urchin for sure.

"Oh no, sir, I came here because Mr. Hall gives me a good meal or two every day. And you know, sir, last week he started even to pay! I get me a shilling a week." He held up his first coin with glee.

"And you like your work?" asked James.

"Of course, sir."

"I'm sure you do. Out here in the woods, no one to trouble you to, and no school to go to either."

"Well, there's a school in New Carlisle, sir," Ben replied, "and a schoolmaster, old Mr. Hobson, but you have to pay for books and such, and I..."

"Your parents don't have the money?" James asked.

"No sir, no parents."

James absorbed the fact: an orphan, here, working in the mill. But then, he knew of plenty of stories of London's orphans — pickpockets and prostitutes. So perhaps this lad was not so badly off.

"Well, Ben," James volunteered on the spur of the moment, "I'll see what I can do about teaching you your L M N O P's."

"Oh, no thank you, sir. All them learning and books — I got no time for that. I gotta earn me money."

"Ben, you can still earn your money. Just maybe in the evenings —"

"Evenings, sir? I don't have no oil lamp nor candle in me tent. How'll I see?"

"Well, maybe I can buy us a candle," James said. "But hold on, I don't even know if I'll be working here."

"Well, sir, you look like a strong man and you look like you've had education. I bet he hires you. He needs a good Number Two man, Mr. Hall does. I've noticed that."

"Oh you have, have you?" James offered. Smart little devil, he thought. No problem to teach him reading and writing. Another reason to hope for the job.

Chapter Seven

As darkness fell, the work stopped. James, with his heart in his mouth and a prayer on his lips, strode into the open end of the mill where the logs were brought in off the river. James selected one man who from his bearing and look — a vigorous short fellow with large ears — must be the owner. "Excuse me, Mr. Hall, sir!"

The man stopped and took James in with a long suspicious look. "What can I do for ye? Come to buy lumber?"

"No sir, in fact, I was looking for work." James spoke firmly even though he felt anything but firm.

"Were ye now?" Mr. Hall gestured for the lantern which one of his men had taken down from its hook on a low beam. "Thank ya, 'Ti-Pete."

James noticed his worn trousers and torn shirt, out at the elbows. Not the look of a rich man, he thought, but then, that was applying Old World standards. Here, clothing meant nothing. He liked that.

"Yes, I am, sir," James added in affirmation, though he hated to push himself. "I'm a hard worker, not afraid of any task. Trained in the British Navy," he added, and then bit his tongue.

"Well," said Mr. Hall, eying him from under bushy eyebrows, "we'll see about that. We work from daylight to dusk. Them's long days now, summer time and all."

"Long days for sure," agreed James, "as I can see now.

But that's just what I need. I would welcome a spell of good hard work." Especially with the news he had just heard back at the Garretts' about Catherine being taken forever, this might get his mind off that piece of ill fortune.

The millwright drew on his pipe and studied James in the low light of a lantern.

"I brought you this letter." James took it from his pocket and handed it to him.

"Who's it from?"

"Mr. Garrett. He thinks I might be of some use, I believe."

"Does he now?" Mr. Hall took the folded parchment, and tore it in pieces. "So William thinks he'll plant the spy in my camp, does he?" He turned with his lantern as though the interview were at an end.

"A spy, sir?" James added quickly, following. "I don't think I understand."

"Don't ye now?" Hall stopped and looked back at him.

James's mind tried to fathom what was being said. "I'm very sorry, Mr. Hall, but I just do not see what you are telling me."

The old man studied him. "How well d'ye know old William?"

"We met briefly two years ago, but then, not again until yesterday. He comes from the north of England as I do, and perhaps he feels some kind of kinship." And then it hit him, William Garrett Sr. must want him out of the way until Catherine and her fiancé could tie the knot. Off here in the woods, James could do little harm. They probably see me, James decided, as a threat to their arranged marriage. But at the moment, he must make every effort to get the job.

He noticed little Ben by his wheelbarrow watching with keen interest. Hall followed his look, and frowned. "Go on with ye now, Ben, get yourself some supper."

Ben turned and walked sheepishly toward the lodgings.

"Actually, sir, I've been chatting with him. I had in mind that if I worked here, I might teach him some reading, writing, and 'rithmatic."

"Now why would ye do that, for pity's sake?"

"Well sir," said James, noticing a hesitation in the millwright, "I know what it is to be uneducated and to be in a class where you're ignored. Everything I learned was from a kindly old tutor who took pity on me and encouraged me to study hard. That's how I came to be, in some small way, an educated man. I'd feel it were my duty to do the same for Ben."

"And I suppose them Garretts saw you as an educated man? And that I could need that kind o' help?"

"No no, sir, they see me, I hope, as a new settler, with dreams for his future, and who is not afraid to work extra hard to realize those dreams."

Hall stared after the men who had gone to their bunkhouse, then pulled out his pipe and tinderbox. He worked at it with the most amazing agility, fingers moving so fast that James could hardly follow him. The tinder was alight in a trice, and from that he lit his pipe.

James felt that Mr. Hall must now be tossed upon the horns of a dilemma: reject James as a spy from his co-owner, William, or accept James as an innocent, and so harness his youthful energy to the sawmill.

James stayed silent. Damn! Why had he given him the letter? Maybe by now the job would be his. He felt oddly as if his thoughts were travelling in some curious link to the millwright's brain.

"Why not just give me a try, sir?" James ventured. "If I prove unworthy, I shall earn nothing. If I succeed, then you will see your output rise in accordance with my hard work." He looked down, nervous lest this last plea had been overdone.

The millwright turned abruptly and started to walk off. James heart sank.

Then he heard Hall call out, "Come with me."

They walked over to a clearing where stood a cabin of rough logs, roofed with overlapping planks. "Had this here built some years ago so the fellas wouldn't have that three-hour walk from Bonaventure every day. French, good workers, though helluva time training them." He shoved open the door.

James saw, in the light of a lantern hung from a beam, four men gathering round an open fireplace in the middle, under a hole in the roof. Kettles and a cauldron hung over the open fire, heating the men's supper. The room contained six rough bunks, much like his lumber camp that winter back of Paspébiac. Here, Hall had provided straw mattresses and the floor was of rough planks, not mud as in the lumber shacks.

"That bunk in the far end — the top one — ye can take that," the millwright said, and made an introduction to his other workers, in French.

So he was hired! James thought. Thank the Good Lord above!

***

"Throw her out o' gear," called the millwright as he hurried down to join James below the heavy flooring of the mill.

Above, 'Ti-Pete slid a lever back, and James heard the system of pulleys and belts slowly wind down. When the whirring stopped, James began to trace the power. He'd always had a yen for mechanical things, although he was new at this sort of work. In the Navy, he had to learn, as had all Midshipmen, the way of sails and jibs and how they worked. And now he marvelled at both the simplicity and complexity of the mill's design beneath the floorboards. Belts and pulleys transferred power from the paddle wheel, through a system of smaller wheels linked by broad belts perhaps six inches wide, to the actual wheel that drove the saw.

"This'll ruin me!" the old man said. "Finish me off. I knew it!"

"No, no, just wait, Mr. Hall. We can fix it. Watch."

Curiously enough, James had only spent ten days at the mill, carrying out boards, rolling logs into place, fastening them for the saw. But once Hall had seen how smart he was, he'd put James in charge of the saw itself whenever he became occupied with customers. This time, James had been hearing a slight difference in the sound of the throb of the cogs and pulleys and, handing over to 'Ti-Pete, he had run below, calling out to Hall.

It wasn't long before they both found it. The main belt had developed a tear that flapped as it careened around the pulleys.

"And wouldn't I be clean out of glue!" Hall sat back disconsolately on the wheelbarrow which Ben had drawn up.

"Well sir, I'd be glad to take a run down to New Carlisle. They must have lots there."

"You're dreaming, laddie. They only make glue in autumn when they butcher the animals. Mostly used up by now." The old man took off his floppy black hat and mopped his forehead. "I knew I should'a been more careful, but already I had four breaks this year." He shook his head sadly. "We're terble behind."

"I can do my best," James said, turning to go. "I'll be back before nightfall."

"You're off now, laddie? Better eat something first."

"No sir, if it's as bad as you say, I'd better be off. We can't shut the mill down for long, or I expect I'll be out of work with the rest of them." He winked at the old fellow, who was now taking considerable cheer at his apprentice's initiative.

***

And so, sooner than expected, James found himself on the trail back to New Carlisle. It was a fine morning and he had time to think as he trotted Indian-style down the wooded trail at a pace learned during his contact with the Micmac. Or at least, dwell on his nightmare: the loss of Catherine. Thoughts of her were better left behind but, like an irritating sore, they kept tormenting him.

Now why is the soul of a man so contrary? he wondered. Why on earth had he set his cap at Catherine, after she'd been taken? But how much that vision of her by the open fire two years before had grown, when down she had come, to waken him with a warning that her brothers were up to no good. That kiss they shared then still haunted him. Now, on the rough track, he longed for those lips again.

Go on, torture yourself, he exclaimed. She'll never be yours. You had your chance and you missed it. Content yourself with the one great love, Magwés, who will never return. Pay Magwés the compliment of being the one and only love of your life. But what about your son, John, back the Port Daniel river with the tribe? Does he not need a surrogate mother? And in his heart of hearts, James knew absolutely that Magwés would want him to have a full life, with a wife and family in which to rear John safely.

So he must learn this new trade at the mill, save his money, and perhaps even bring his mother over. That might be a good way to manage having his son with him: she could look after him of course. But would trading the comparative luxury of Raby Castle for this harsh wilderness life be in her best interest? Well, just leave that choice to her. At any rate, he must get on and write a proper letter, and get it off on the next schooner.

Then how should he deal with losing Catherine? Might he find some way to repair the damage? Might she talk the whole thing over? Not much hope there, alas. Stymied again.

Chapter Eight

"So what on earth are you doing?" Catherine asked. Bent over and carrying a boulder, she seemed shocked to see James in her field.

James stood tongue-tied. "I didn't expect to see you here, Catherine. I came to find William."

Catherine dropped her stone on the growing rock pile at one side of the field. "My father has gone to Bonaventure. The boys are in the back field, picking stones there, too." She turned back to the field for more rocks. "Did you not get the job at the mill?"

James had to grin. "He's keeping me, heaven knows why."

"I had heard, I confess. So why are you here now?"

He found himself falling in beside her as she strode out toward the next big rock. "We need glue. And good stitching. One of our main pulleys is about to go." When she picked up a rock, James got an even larger one and they both headed back to the rock pile. "I went to the house, but found no one."

They dropped their rocks and walked out for more.

"Who do you think has the best glue in town?" He stooped to pick up another. "I tried the general store, but he is out of it. The storekeeper suggested I ask the neighbours around, to see who's been making glue recently." They picked a few more stones and headed for the rock pile.

"I think we have some somewhere, left over from last year." She dropped her rock on to the pile.

"I also need some sturdy material to stitch onto the main belt." They returned for more stones, their movements forming a rhythmical pattern as they laboured under the almost clear sky.

"I think we may have some stitching also." She stooped for another stone. "So you can sew? I have a hole in one of my blouses..."

"Send it along! James Alford, tailor and profiteer!" He picked up a heavy rock and hefted it back to the stone pile. "How long ago did your family clear this?" He meant, of course, clear the land of trees.

"Before I was born. But every time we plough, we turn up more rocks. I don't know where they all come from. This field is the worst. Too busy to clear it this last while, what with all the work over on our other land."

"You do a lot of this?"

She nodded. "Even little Eleanor picks stones, the smaller ones, but she's needed at home to help Mama." They brought several more stones back to the pile. "I suppose this work you're doing with me means you expect to be invited to eat once again..."

He glanced at her, to divine her intent: teasing him? Or being nasty. "No expectations." But then he added quickly, "Lots of hopes."

"What's that supposed to mean?"

James kept silent.

She went on: "If wishes were horses, then beggars would ride."

They worked on in silence. After a bit James asked, "So when is the wedding?"

"Not sure."

Was that a glimmer of hope? "Billy will be a very lucky man. I hope he is worthy of you."

"I think it's more a question of — will I be worthy of him?"

"Ridiculous!" James said. "Who thinks that?"

"Everyone. They don't see me, I'm afraid, the way you do."

"And how do I see you?" James teased.

She remained silent.

"All right, so how do they see you?"

"Too headstrong. I won't put up with balderdash!"

"Oh-oh, I'd better watch out." At the same time, Catherine grew in his estimation. Working hard on the farm, doing a man's work, and even now, able to divine his inner feelings. Don't give up any pursuit right now, he told himself, as the glue and stitching went right out of his mind.

"Oh, for that," Catherine interrupted, "use the rock sled. It's up there in the corner."

"All right." He trotted off, got the sled, manhandled the heavy stone onto it and hauled it across to the pile.

When he rejoined her, he said, "The way I see it, there's not a man alive who isn't a hundred times better off with a wife. Any wife," he added, so as not to be too pointed.

Catherine smiled.

"Oh yes, any wife at all," he went on a bit desperately, "let her be cross-eyed or bow-legged —"

"Thank you, kind sir!" She curtseyed and smiled as she went for more stones. "Cross-eyed and bow-legged indeed."

"Indeed." Then James flung caution aside, and allowed himself to overstep the bounds of propriety. "Though I confess, at the risk of incurring wrath for being 'full of balderdash,' I find you the most attractive woman on the whole Gaspé Coast." Oh-oh, stop that, he commanded himself. But for the life of him, he could not. "Any man who gets you would find himself lifted onto an unparalleled earthly paradise!"

She looked to him sharply. He caught the look. "Oh, forgive me. I did forget that you were betrothed."

"Indeed you did!" She turned quickly away. They worked on in silence again.

Fortunately a cool breeze was, as usual, blowing in off the bay. Nonetheless, it was hot work and heavy for a girl, James thought. But the more he worked beside her, the more attractive she grew. What would he give to have her working on his own farm?

After a period of silence, Catherine suddenly stopped and faced him. "If you feel that, truly feel that, and you're not just full of blather like any besotted Irishman —"

"I'm not Irish, I'm British."

"Whatever you are, if there were any meaning to your words, you would have come back sooner. You would not have stayed away so long." He saw that the blood was rising into her face and her eyes were beginning to flash. "Have you any idea what last summer was like for me? Expecting you to appear at any moment?"

What was she saying? And with such emotion, it did seem to come right from the heart. Could she really mean that? Could she really have been waiting for him? "I wanted to, Catherine, but —"

"More blather! I thought from our one meeting that I

could trust you." She turned back to stone hunting. "I misjudged you, that's all. It was my own fault. Don't feel badly. I have learned my lesson. Well and truly!"

James pondered a reply as they dropped their stones. When she straightened, she looked him straight in the eye. "I think it best you go now. You can check for glue with the cabinet- maker, if you have not already done so. I'm sure he will have some." Her eyes were flashing. "I can finish this field myself very easily, thank you very much. When I get home, I'll leave on the porch some material for you, and whatever glue I can find. But please don't knock."

"You want me to leave now? Right now?"

"Yes. You disturb me, far too much." Was she close to tears? "And that, if you must know, is the one thing I most hate to admit." She turned away, and headed off, stopping to add, "I don't like men coming around, talking me up, without an honest idea in their heads. Except perhaps one, which all men have, I'm finding out. Just one single thought, all of them, and one I do not relish."

James took off his hat and wiped his brow. This was far worse than he expected. How could he make it right?

A thousand strands of feeling tangled up his brain: How could he explain? He should definitely not tell her the real reason he'd not returned last summer, apart from clearing his land, was that he had been betrothed.

He cast down his eyes, dropped the boulder he was carrying onto the rock pile, and began to walk away. But his last glance at her eyes flashing so angrily under the sweaty hair hanging down under the kerchief made her utterly desirable — now, when she was at her most angry.

He quickened his pace. How else to regain any dignity? How else to show he meant it, but to take off with speed.

Had he looked back, he would have seen her shapely form slump, her hands drop the rocks in the middle of the field, and turn away, hands covering her face as emotions welled.

He entered the trees, and paused. Would he ever see her again? Yes, of course, but only from a distance. Would he ever have another time alone with her? Not if she could help it. She did not want him around; he disturbed her too much.

But then again, no time like the present. Here and now, he faced his last, and only, chance to confront her. He could not let it go. He turned.

He saw her stoop and pick up the stones she had dropped and walk heavily over to the pile, where she let them fall once again, oblivious of him, of everything, even of the stones themselves.

He stepped out from the trees and covered the ground quickly toward her, holding up one hand to stop her speaking.

"Catherine," he said stoutly, "every word I have spoken to you — how I feel about you, about us — and I know I shouldn't say it, but every word is true, I swear on my mother's head."

She stared at him, angry, but moisture springing into her eyes.

"Now I know," he went on, "you would rather I left this minute. But I intend to spend the afternoon here clearing stones. Forget for a moment the past — let us just share one afternoon alone together. For had fate been otherwise, the Good Lord might have arranged for us to do this for the rest of our natural lives. I want just this one afternoon to remember."

She glanced at him, then lowered her eyes, perhaps so that he would not see any tears start, and turned away. "All right, this one last time, let us work together."

***

Heart soaring, James fell easily into his Indian run. Dusk would soon be falling; a dangerous time to be heading back to this trail. Why on earth had he left it so late? He had been warned about thieves, so now, he was on the alert. He had to get this glue from the cabinet-maker's and stitching from the Garretts back as quickly as possible. But no point in running so fast as to collide with danger.

His body was bursting with feelings for Catherine. Such a glorious afternoon, working side by side with her for those few cherished hours. Time wasted? Not in the slightest. Because getting to know her would sustain him over the many weeks of summer as he laboured in the mill. The days would be so long, he knew. But perhaps another chance would present itself.

He stopped to listen. Voices ahead? As he stood panting, he became sure. Two men, laughing. Now what?

He waited. Were they coming toward him? Or was he overtaking them? From the odd sounds of their broken conversation, they were staying in one spot. Not good.

Better not risk it. This glue and this stitching were vital. He turned into the deeper woods.

Again, he blessed his Micmac friends for their moccasins that allowed him to move through the undergrowth silently. He picked his way carefully past thickets and through bushes, going around the thieves waiting, perhaps, to pounce.

He stopped again. The voices had grown quiet, as if they had heard him. Silence lay like the dusk around them. He didn't move. And apparently, neither did they.

After a time, their voices began again. Did they suspect a deer, a bear, even a moose? Had he been successful? Reaching the trail, he set off again at his swift Indian pace; he wanted no more impediments to his getting that glue and stitching to the mill.

Chapter Nine

Delighted with the success of James's mission, Mr. Hall watched him repair the belt for the main pulley in his tent, a ways off from the other cabin. Hall allowed as how he much preferred this solitary existence — feelings James shared. The whale oil lamp beside them on a stump threw a glow onto Ben's swarthy face as he sat watching with dark eyes.

One end was now glued, stitched, and beeswaxed, and the second one lay before them. Mr. Hall pulled at it to test it. "You're better 'n any of us. You'll make a fine millwright one day."

James set to stitching the other end, wearing his "palm," a heavy leather covering for his hand with a loop for the thumb. He thrust his sailor's awl, about four inches long, rounded at the eye, into the heavy canvas of the belt. "Well, 'tis a farmer I'll want to be, sir, although I certainly enjoy this time here at the mill."

"A farmer, is it?"

"Yes sir, I have a modest piece of land and I am about to start on my new house. I have the foundation prepared, rocks from the brook, but next I need lumber."

"So that's why ye want boards from me instead of all cash?"

James nodded.

"I can see ye done yer bit o' stitching in the Navy."

"Aye. You can't work in the Navy as long as I did without learning something of all that. Our uniforms — I was a Midshipman — had to be just so, you know. No mother or wife to sew it. And then, of course, there's the sails which I seldom touched, tarpaulins and such like. I'd watch the sail-makers work on them; I guess I never knew when it might come in handy."

Hall turned to the lad who was solemnly taking it all in. "You're larning from a master, Ben."

"Indeed I am, sir." From the way Ben looked at James, he almost worshipped this ex-seaman rapidly becoming Hall's Number Two.

"I enjoy teaching him, sir," said James, finding it helpful to divert his mind from those blue eyes that followed him through the days. On the practical side, he doubted lovely Sorrel with her tiny frame and hunched shoulders could ever take the arduous winters in a desolate and isolated cabin, much as she had also impressed him. No, it was Catherine he wanted, nay, longed for.

"Them Garretts is a fine family." Mr. Hall seemingly had read the thoughts behind his foreman's distant eyes. "Byes, that old Will sure has the pair of prettiest daughters in New Carlisle."

James looked up sharply. Well, he'd grown to like Hall, so why not confide to him some of his buried feelings?

"Yes sir, I've been far and wide on His Majesty's ships, but never have I seen anyone to compare with the young Catherine." He dropped his eyes as he took the next piece of belt and prepared it for stitching. "I've never met Billy Brotherton, but I presume he must be of a calibre equal to or even greater than she, for William Garrett to have granted this match."

James glanced up to see a curious look come onto the older man's face. But without pursuing the matter, he continued stitching in silence, thrusting the needle even more angrily than needed.

After a time, Mr. Hall spoke. "Them Brothertons, I had a bit of problem with them, so you can't count on me for any true appraisal of Billy." James looked up. "But the one thing all of us know, that Billy is one spoiled brat. Always was. My son went to school with him. Nobody liked him. 'Cept for a bunch of fools followed him as leader. Terble good athlete. That kinda made up for things, I guess."

"Get the glue ready, Ben," was all James said in reply.

"I reckon she'd be better off with the likes of a man like you," Hall averred, "a man who's served his good King for years in the Navy, and who's not afraid of hard work. But that's just my opinion."

"I only wish to God it were hers too, sir," mumbled James as reached for the glue pot. But later that night as he lay on his straw mattress, James tossed and turned in agony. Come on, he scolded, forget Catherine. Work with them all here at the mill, and teach young Ben. There'll be lots of young girls come along, once you've got your house built.

But he knew that wasn't true; he knew he was just lying to himself. After much anguish, his worn-out body drove him to sleep.

***

A month later, the squeal of the saw could not drown out the agonized cry as a stream of red liquid spun into the air, covering James as he stood in the millwright's position. He threw the saw out of gear, and grabbed up Ben where he had fallen.

These sounds and spray of blood were to be replayed in his mind for many months to come. But now, he hurried out holding the lad, his brain reeling as he cried for help.

'Ti-Pete came running, calling to his mate, Serge, out on the floating logs, who in spite of his girth came leaping across like a squirrel.

James kneeled, placed Ben on the earth, tore off his shirt and tied one sleeve around the arm as a tourniquet. Lifting his shirt, he wiped his own eyes clear of the blood. "Get Mr. Hall!"

"Gone upriver," 'Ti-Pete replied.

James looked down at the boy, his eyes clouding over, stricken with shock. Dazed and clearly in another world, Ben's face bore only a questioning expression: how had this happened?

During the four or five weeks since they had repaired the main belt, James had found himself increasingly in the position of Number Two. And so he had occasionally invited Ben into this main sawing area to see how it all worked, as part of Ben's general education.

That morning, Hall told James he had noticed a small malfunction — every so often, as the log was hefted closer to the saw after each plank had been sheared off and kicked out, it gave a jolt. Hall had decided they should try to fix it after nightfall, so as not to shut down the mill at the height of activity. Today he'd gone off to Bonaventure to try and find a carpenter who might help them, and left the mill to James. The board had flung up, struck Ben on the head, knocked him backwards and then, as he grabbed for support, his arm had come against the sharp heavy-toothed saw blade.

Act fast. The blood came pumping in spurts out of the mangled forearm and wrist and fingers. How much of his arm could be saved?

Auguste, a tall, long-faced worker, and Serge, the burly log-jumper, rushed up. "A strip of finer cloth!" James cried, repeating it in French. "I need a better tourniquet."

Auguste hurried off. James thought fast: Get him to a doctor? What doctor? No doctor that he knew of in New Carlisle — three hours away on foot. And they had no horse available anyway. The realization struck him — no one else. He would have to handle this alone. Think fast, but think clearly. A life was at stake.

Auguste returned with a strip of cloth. James tied it quickly around the arm, picked up a firm twig, thrust it into the bandage and wound it tight. "You're going to be fine, Ben, just fine."

He hoped Ben's state of shock would keep him still while he thought out his next move. The battles he had seen on the *Bellerophon* should serve him now. In one of them, he had assisted the ship's surgeon. He made himself look down with a professional eye at the boy's arm. Fingers sliced off, hand mangled, wrist torn apart, exposing the bone in a mass of raw flesh and white tendons. The tourniquet had to be released every ten minutes or so. What next?

One thing was certain: no way to save the hand. Amputation? Inside, his stomach churned. He loved the little lad. What lay ahead might turn the stomach of any grown man — even a surgeon. Nothing for it, he had to amputate.

"Light a fire," he ordered, and Auguste hurried off. Then, to 'Ti-Pete, "Go into the mill, ready the saw right away." 'Ti-Pete jumped to obey: the command was given with such force and alacrity, as when James had commanded his gun crew.

"Ben," he said, looking into the hazy eyes, "you'll have to trust me. In half an hour, it will all be over, and you'll go to sleep. I was in the Navy, Ben, I have seen it many times. You'll soon be fine." He knew that telling a lie was the best thing he could do, in the circumstances.

Ben nodded. "Water," he mumbled.

"Water!" James commanded, and as he picked the boy up, a container was duly brought. "And rum! A flagon of rum."

Serge ran back to the bunkhouse. The saw had been thrust into gear, and its whine grew. James looked down at the little lad in his arms. Quickly, before he thought too much about it, he picked him up and headed into the mill where the logs were hauled up the inclined planks.

Ben must have sensed what was going to happen, for he started to squirm. "No!" He screamed and clutched fiercely at James.

"Ben, this will be quick."

"No no no," yelled the boy. He struggled in James's arms, with fighting strength.

"Help me!" James demanded. 'Ti-Pete quickly tightened his grip on the lad.

"Ben, be brave. We've got to. It will save your life."

The rum appeared. "Drink this, Ben." James motioned

for 'Ti-Pete to lie him on the wood platform in front of the long slicing saw. He put the bottle to his lips, and the lad, looking up into James's face, took a swig and grimaced. "More Ben, more, it will help." He drank a few slugs, coughing and spluttering.

Auguste came up. *"Le feu, ça va."*

"The fire's going? Good." James grabbed Serge and whispered in French, "Look, we've got to amputate. You'll hold his arm against the saw. 'Ti-Pete will work the saw. I'll help you. You'll have to hold him tight, the arm tight, otherwise it won't be a clean slice. Use all your strength."

Serge stared in surprise, even horror.

"Think you can do it?" James looked into his eyes.

Serge stood silent, stricken with doubt. Then he nodded, clenched his fist and held it up, indicating his readiness.

"Good," James said. "Let's go fast."

To Auguste, who was standing by, still stunned at what was about to happen, he ordered, "Go back, check the fire in the cabin. Stick in our shovel. I need it red hot. Quickly!"

Auguste turned and ran out. "All right." James gestured to Serge. "Pay no attention to anything. Just do what has to be done."

"Oui oui, je fais mon possible." Serge picked up Ben, who writhed vigorously, twisting in his arms. But big Serge, obviously a father with children of his own, spoke in calming French as he tightened his grip. He stepped beside the saw.

With stomach falling through his boots, James reached out and took the mangled arm. "Quickly!"

Ignoring Ben's cries, in one clean swoop, Serge and

James placed the arm against the saw and the blade sliced cleanly through the forearm, quicker than ever James had imagined. He let the discarded hand drop. Then he raced around to the other side of the saw where Ben screamed and stout Serge looked as if he might faint.

James grabbed Ben from his arms. "It's done, Ben, it's done." He carried the swooning lad quickly outside, laid him on the grass, and set about loosening the tourniquet. Serge came out to stand beside him.

The blood streamed out. He let it flow for a moment and then tightened it again, stanching the flow.

"Where's that shovel?" he asked. Serge shook his head. James looked toward the cabin, then gathered Ben in his arms. Ben had sunk into deeper shock as they hurried into the bunkhouse. Just as well.

Auguste sat heating the shovel in the fire. James laid Ben on the nearest lower bunk and motioned for 'Ti-Pete to hold him. He spoke into the lad's eyes. "Ben," he said, "it's almost over." He prayed hard for God to give him the strength. "When you wake up, you'll be fine."

Just then, one of Hall's customers from New Carlisle came by, calling out in a broad Scot's accent, "Where are yae all?" He stopped in the doorway as he saw the men.

"Won't be long, sir." James came over and checked the shovel, already glowing.

The Scotsman stepped in and stood aghast.

"Hello, Sir," James called. "We've had an accident. You'll have to wait."

"Angus Maclean. But can I help ye?" James noticed his strong, freckled forearms and firm blue eyes under his sandy hair.

"No thank you, Mr. Maclean." He turned. "Now Auguste, give me that shovel. I'll have to press it against Ben's stump."

Angus stepped forward, his fearful eyes wide with horror. "Ye cannae. I will nae allow it!"

"Mr. Maclean," James said flatly, "it's our only chance. Cauterize the stump. I've done it in the Navy."

"Look!" Maclean's voice rose. "The boy's got no hand!"

"I had to amputate. Now he must not see this coming. Moments like this, a man has ten times his strength. We've got to do it without him knowing." He turned to Auguste. "I've seen dying men take four others to hold them down. We must be quick! No slip ups. That red-hot shovel goes cleanly and fast against his stump. Understood? Are you with me?"

Angus lowered his eyes, sighed, and then lifted them. "Dear Lord, ha'e a bit of mercy."

"Ben oui. Je suis là."

"Cover Ben's face with a blanket," James ordered. "Quickly. Hold him, Serge."

Serge leapt to do as he was told. James peered at the shovel. Yes. Glowing red. Flashes of his own trauma when he'd been attacked by a cougar and Magwés cauterized him almost blinded him. He remembered he had passed out with the pain. Would Ben do the same? Such brutal punishment.

The shovel shone scarlet. The men were strong, their arms toughened by years of heaving logs: they would brook no resistance.

"Hold his stump, and hold it hard," James ordered. "I'll be quick." He jerked his head, and Auguste came over to help the other two.

Angus put his hands to his face and turned away.

Auguste felt for Ben's arm, thrust it into the air. Ben gave no resistance, not seeing what was coming.

James took the glowing metal and in two steps crossed the space. Before any of them really knew what was happening, he placed it against the stump.

Amidst a loud hiss of steaming blood, Ben gave an unearthly wail and slumped. The smell of burning flesh filled the room. James took the shovel back, threw it by the fire, and straightened. The men relaxed their grip and stood up, panting. Ben had passed out. They took the blanket from his face and covered his tiny body.

Angus Maclean turned back. "Heavenly Lord, I've seen a miracle."

James shook his head. Then, matter of factly: "Now, let's us all polish off that bottle of rum."

Chapter Ten

James cradled Ben in a blanket in his arms as they bumped swiftly over the wooded trail back to New Carlisle. His companion and driver was none other than Billy Brotherton.

After they had all taken their slug of rum, with Ben passed out, James had set off for New Carlisle at his Indian trot, covering the miles quicker than ever. Over the weeks, he had taken to running beside the river to check on the latest log booms floating down. The exercise gave him time to think — anything to avoid sitting and moping all day about his lost love. So he was again in the best of shape.

Someone had to be found who could look after Ben. Mr. Hall's family was away visiting Quebec City, and the other owner was William Garrett. So it was to the Garretts that James ran, arriving on their doorstep out of breath and in a sweat.

They were all out but Mrs. Garrett, who welcomed him with astonishment. "Whatever is wrong?" she gasped, opening the door and ushering James inside. Once he had caught his breath and sipped a cup of tea that she had hastily prepared, together with a slice of bread and molasses, he told her the awful story as calmly as he could.

"I have to find a family to look after Ben for two or three weeks until his arm heals. He needs lots of nourishment and sleep, and I'm not sure where to turn."

"Well, you've come to the right place," Mrs. Garrett declared. "We shall definitely look after the poor wee orphan."

James looked up at her with softened eyes. "Thank you, Mrs. Garrett," he said, biting into another slice of bread and molasses, "Thank you so much. I had hoped you might."

So his first mission had been successful. The next problem was articulated by her before he got the words out of his mouth: "But James, however would you get him here? Mr. Hall has no means of bringing him."

"No, ma'am, I was hoping to find someone here in New Carlisle who had a fast horse and a buggy."

"Let me think." Mrs. Garrett sat for a moment, sipping the tea which she had poured for herself when preparing a cup for James. "You know, I believe the Brothertons have just bought a new sulky."

"What on earth is that?" James asked.

She smiled: everyone knew what a sulky was. "Well, it has two big round wheels with a seat between, and is meant for speed. I think Billy persuaded his father to get it. They give him everything he wants, you know."

James nodded calmly, but the words stabbed him like a Spanish stiletto. She went to her drawer and took out pen, ink, and some parchment. "Take this note at once." While writing, she gave James directions to the Brothertons.

And so it was that he got a ride back, picked up Ben, and was now sitting beside his nemesis, Billy Brotherton, on their way to New Carlisle.

Both ways, Billy had blathered on about his fast horse

and his new sulky, and some horse races he'd gotten his father to organize. But now, on the way back, he broached the subject of Catherine. "And ye know," he said, "I'll soon be married."

"Oh?" responded James. "Who to?" He didn't want to let on he knew anything.

"Byes, a fine woman," Billy went on. "Can't wait to get her into the sheets." He grinned at James.

James repressed the urge to knock him out of the fast-moving carriage. "You still haven't told me who it is."

"Why it's that juicy young Catherine Garrett. Can't wait to haul her into bed. Pretty wild one, too. Do ye know her?"

"I've met her," James responded. "But she didn't strike me as particularly wild."

"It's that look in her eye," said Billy "She'll give me the ride o' me life, I bet. And I don't mean in the sulky." He leered at James. "She'll be a real wild one once I get her under me blankets."

James stomach turned. With a great effort of will, he kept himself still. "And when is this wild ride of yours going to happen?"

"The sooner the better," said Billy, "but she don't seem too anxious to bed down just yet." He paused, licking his lips. "So maybe I'll have t'wait till spring."

Better play into it, thought James, hating this whole conversation. You'll find out more that way.

Billy looked over at him. "I heard you was a sailor. Bet you had lots of juicy stuff in port. I heard about you sailors," he leered.

"I might have had my share," affirmed James, playing along.

"I get my pick of the girls around here," said Billy, "but they ain't none as nice as that there Catherine. Can't wait to get my hands on them big breasts of hers. I'll soon show her what's what."

James felt his fists clench. It took a tremendous effort of will to stop them from smashing into Billy's face. "Well, I wish you the best of luck."

"Tell me where ya live," said Bill, "and I'll see you're invited to the wedding. Big affair, I promise ya."

"I'm sure it will be." Just then Ben stirred. He had been in a semi-coma.

"Amazing he can sleep like 'at with his hand off. How did ya say it got cut?"

"I sawed it off," said James coldly. "Then I pressed a red hot shovel against the stump, to cauterize it."

Billy looked him with some admiration. This was a sailor not to tangle with.

"Gave him something to make him sleep better, and something else to lessen the pain," James said. "Found it on my run to New Carlisle."

"Now there's a funny thing," said Billy. "What was it? Laudanum? How'd ya get it on your run?"

"Oh, there wasn't any Laudanum back at the mill and anyway, I think these herbs are more effective."

"What kind of herbs are they?" asked Billy.

"Just some medicine I learned from the Micmac."

Billy swung his head sideways. "What! You mix with them Injuns? Bloody animals! Me friends and me went lookin' for some to pick off with shotguns. Never found none. They knew well enough to stay away. Came after us English real good, I heard, after we beat the bloody French in Nova Scotia. 'Afore I was born."

For the first time in his life, James felt a real sense of loathing. How could he let this brute near his beloved Catherine? But what could he do? Mrs. Garrett liked the Brothertons.

***

The speeding sulky rattled down a New Carlisle street toward the Garretts'. Word had obviously spread and several out on their verandas waved a greeting. Billy, of course, sat up and, as appropriate for the hero of the day, waved back. James silently cradled the dazed Ben under a blanket.

When they drew up in front of the Garrett house, the family had gathered on the veranda. Catherine hurried down to greet them, followed by Eleanor. William rose from his rocking chair, a stout and sturdy figure with his cane. The three boys leapt down, William Jr. to hold the horse, John to help James with his burden, and the third, little Joseph, running off to fetch some oats at his father's command.

"Byes, we made terble fast time," Billy said, pleased at all the attention. "She's the best horse around. There's nawthin' anywhere'd beat her. I just gave her the head and she ran fer't."

James eyed Catherine as he handed her his patient. How could she be so fooled by this idiot? Catherine just carried Ben in her arms up the steps, followed by her mother.

"Well, come in come in," William welcomed them both.

"Come, take a load off your feet, Billy," Eleanor added.

"I bet ye could do with a cup of tea after that long drive."

"That I could, ma'am, thank you. It's not often I get a chance to save a life like this." He walked up the veranda stairs. James stood by the horse, drained but relieved that Ben was now in good hands.

"Come on then, James, you'll join us, surely." Mr. Garrett waved him into the house.

James stood for a moment and then turned to look up. "I'm sorry, sir, but they need me back at the mill. I'd better get going."

"Come come, James," William muttered, clapping his hand on Billy's shoulder as he came in the door. "Surely they'd give you time for a cuppa tea before you left. I'll see if I can rustle up someone with a horse to take you back. Young Billy's here has had his fill for the moment, I'm sure. Just give us time."

"Time is what I don't have, sir," said James. "But thank you kindly, and please tell the missus I'm very grateful for the invitation. But I will be back to see Ben, of course. Make sure he knows he's not forgotten. Next Sunday for sure." And James turned away, wondering how he would endure that next Sunday being close to Catherine and yet knowing so much more about the dreadful future to which she had been condemned.

And then, with anguish in his soul, he forced himself to turn away and set off at a gentle trot which he could keep up for hours on end. Had he looked back, he would have seen in the eyes of Joseph, and John, and indeed their father pausing in his doorway, a look of admiration that was clear to behold.

Chapter Eleven

Three Sundays later after supper, the Garretts with their special guest, James, and their adopted orphan, Ben, pushed back their chairs and came to sit round the great stone fireplace. Dusk was approaching; this first week in September, temperatures had begun to drop and the evenings were chill enough that the fire provided a comfort. The two oldest brothers had gone off with a caution from their father to be sure and stay away from the demon rum. He would check their breath on re-entering, and severe would be his punishment for any who transgressed.

They had persuaded James to stay, an exception for him. Last week when he had come to see Ben, he had left before supper, unable to put himself through the pain of being with Catherine. But this Sunday, he had gotten so caught up teaching Ben arithmetic in his upstairs room, he hadn't noticed the hour. Too late to extricate himself without appearing rude, he had accepted.

No sooner had they settled themselves than William, his eyes shrewdly staring over half lenses, peered at James. "Well, James, the whole of New Carlisle has been talking about ye."

James lifted his eyes. "Really sir? How so?"

Mrs. Garrett gave a laugh. "Now come, James, surely

you've heard. Everyone is quite in awe of how you came to save little Benigno's life."

"Who?" asked James. "Is that his real name?"

"Yes. He's Portuguese, it appears, poor little lad."

"Aye, you showed fortitude and coolness under fire, young man. Deserving of a medal, if this were Ticonderoga." William grinned at his own reference to the last battle he had been in.

"Oh no, it was nothing. Really."

"Come along, James, you're among friends," William prodded. "I have no doubt you learned all that in the Navy."

"Well, I suppose, in part, sir." He had studiously avoided looking at Catherine all evening, and now she was making it difficult, sitting right across from him, hands folded in her lap, watching his every move.

"You must've seen action, m'boy, when ye were aboard that ship, what was it called?"

"We called it the *Billy Ruffian*, sir, but her proper name was the *Bellerophon*."

"Ah yes, lot o' talk of the *Bellerophon* these weeks," William replied.

"Oh yes? How so?"

"Well, you must know she carried the Emperor Napoleon back to England this July."

James turned pale, and remained motionless. "The Emperor Napoleon. Sir, I don't quite understand. We beat him?"

"Aye, mighty Wellington at the Battle of Waterloo, and you fellows at sea, finally, we had him blockaded and cornered in the Bay of Biscay. He went and gave himself up, aye, he did that. The *Bellerophon* took him to good old

England, him and his bloody lot of Frenchmen."

"But this is most astonishing, sir. What happened when they got to England?"

"No news yet. Only just happened, y'see. July."

James could hardly contain his thoughts. Ever since the Battle of the Glorious First of June in 1794, Napoleon had been their enemy and their quarry. The *Bellerophon* had been ordered into the Baltic Sea because all the great pine for navy spars and the tar came through Baltic ports which the French had been blockading. James had also spent a couple of years cruising the coast of France, trying to hem in the French fleet. And he'd lived through harsh battles, the greatest being Alexandria and Trafalgar, and survived. It quite took the wind out of his sails, as the saying goes, to find out that England was no longer at war. "And I missed being there to see all that? The Emperor himself!"

"Aye. Would you like to be back in the Service, then?"

"Oh no sir, not for a moment. But still, it must have been a thrilling experience for my shipmates. After all the fighting they've seen, with him and his ships."

"Aye, it would that. So you've seen some battles, have ye?"

"Well sir, I suppose I have..." James could see what William was getting at, and he was not at all sure he wanted to open up those old wounds.

"Now come on laddie, don't be shy. You know a lot about naval warfare, I warrant."

"Well, a little, sir," said James modestly. He avoided looking at the two women who were watching keenly.

"Go on."

"Well, I suppose the worst battle I've been in," he said,

"was off the Coast of Spain. Whenever I think of my time in the Navy, that's about what I remember: Trafalgar. In that battle, our ship took a proper beating. And now they picked her to transfer the Emperor himself!" James shook his head.

"Quite a time ago though, them battles?"

"Seems like yesterday, sir. In Alexandria, 1798, fifty-seven dead, one hundred and thirty-eight wounded. We had to be towed back to England for repairs."

"The *Bellerophon* beaten by a French fleet." William blew out smoke in a snort and leaned forward.

"Oh no, our Navy beat them finally, sir, but —"

"How come, if you lot had to be towed home?"

"Well, we had ten ships of the line to their thirteen, they outnumbered us, but...," he paused. No harm in telling his side of the story; it might help him get it out of his system forever. "The French fleet were anchored in Aboukir Bay and Admiral Nelson gave the orders, and with our wind aft, we sailed right for them, in a single file."

"And you right up there on deck?"

"Oh no sir, my main station was a gun deck. 32s. I had command of seven. Twenty-eight in all."

"What's a 32?" Catherine asked.

"It fires thirty-two-pound shot," he replied, without looking at her. "But the explosions were still deafening. On the deck above, that's our 18s, another twenty-eight, which fire eighteen-pound shot. Each cannon needs lots of men — not counting the lads who run up and down with the powder. You see," he said, warming to the tale, "you've got to drop in the powder, and then the heavy shot, stog the wad with a great ramrod, draw the gun up to the gunport, light the touch-hole, lots going on."

"How exciting!"

"Well, exciting till you get in a fight, ma'am. Then..." James trailed off, finding himself disturbed at the visions that arose before him.

"Then what?" Catherine asked.

"Leave him be, Catherine," her mother urged.

"No, she's right to ask. You're all correct to want to know. It's terrible. War. Battles. Mr. Garrett knows. The carnage is just..." James went on in a low voice. "Men working next to me were blown to smithereens. Bits of arm, legs, brains spewed out. Blood running down the deck. Shrapnel, splinters from the wood, it wreaks havoc with your flesh, you bleed even when you don't feel it." He lapsed into silence, before clearing his throat and going on. "You see, we were drawn up right against *l'Orient* — the biggest French ship, double the firepower — and she just towered above us. Her marines, posted high up the mizzen and main mast platforms, they just raked our decks with firepower. And their cannonry, they had one hundred and twenty-four guns to our seventy-four, and heavier, it was awful. Booming explosions, smoke everywhere, and dark too, deafening, but we kept on firing! They poured it on, and so did we. Not sure how or why the Good Lord spared me. But I shall never forget... one of my gunners." He didn't raise his head, but stared fixedly at the floor, missing the looks of dismay on Eleanor and Catherine's faces.

"Our captain, Darby, he was hit early, knocked unconscious, the first mate Lt. Daniel, he was killed, London, the Second Officer, and Fourth and Fifth Lieutenants, all dead. I remember at Trafalgar, Wemyss, the Marine Captain, he had his leg blown off. He said, 'A mere scratch! I apologize for having left the deck on such a trifling occasion,' or something like that. Imagine. He died right after.

"Discipline, we worked hard, we worked well, the men were just amazing, you know, unbelievable how they kept going, so many of their mates beside them cut to pieces." He warmed to the subject. "A fire was started on our lower deck, right near the powder room. You know what that means? One of my gunners got a bunch of men together, and they worked the hand pump to put it out — Captain himself didn't even know, nor anyone on the top deck. Cause a panic if they knew beforehand. Y'see, we'd been enmeshed with *l'Orient,* and a fire started on her, too, blazing high, we all saw it, we tried to get free but our mizzen mast had fallen, then our main, so we strung up our jib, and just managed with a bit of wind to haul away.

"And then, my God, up that ship went, I don't think I've ever heard anything like it, lit up the whole sky, a noise you cannot imagine, the whole ship, sailors and all, blown to hell. We'd made it just in time. Otherwise we'd all have gone sky high with them, the whole bloody lot of us. But of course, though we were saved, the *Billy Ruffian* didn't fare so well. Blood running everywhere, our guns were thrown off their carriages, gunners cut into pieces, all at night too, just a few lanterns, no good really, and bright flashes of the guns, dead dragged out of the way so we could keep going... deafening noise, our cannon and theirs, all going off together."

"But did you beat them, finally?"

"Oh yes sir, we licked them. The fleet did. Us, we were drifting, pretty helpless at the end, highest casualties in the battle, too," he said, with a touch of pride, but also with a deep sorrow as it all rolled over him once again. "I have no desire to boast, but it was well said that the coolness and efficiency of the British sailor under fire allowed us to snatch our victory."

"But your gunner, you were telling us," Catherine asked.

"Oh yes. There was a tremendous noise — part of the gun port was torn away just as we fired. I heard through the smoke and chaos, a cry, and when I could see, one of my gunners, my favourite, actually, he was lying back, dead, I thought. Where his left arm had been... just a mangled stump. Pouring blood.

"I grabbed him up, ordered the rest to keep firing and, as someone who could be spared — you need all the crew to fire — and half carried, half dragged him down to the cockpit, that's where we Middies slept: our Surgeon, Dr. Bellamy, had made it into his surgery, below the water line. Covered our table with a sheet.

"My gunner came to in my arms, but I could tell he wasn't fully conscious, his eyes flickering, his blood running over both of us. I tried to clutch his arm in a way that would stop the bleeding. Please, I prayed, please let him live. But I knew that although my Maker had been very good at answering every prayer, this was one he would be hard put to grant.

"'You're going to be fine,' I told him, as we started down the companionway. 'Lots of sailors have only one arm, don't worry. You'll be taken for our good Admiral Nelson, you watch!' As you may know, our commander had lost his arm in the battle at Tenerife. 'We'll get you to the sawbones, and he'll make you right as rain.' I knew that Dr. Bellamy would have to perform a miracle, but then, they do happen, don't they?

"At any rate, I laid him on the sacking outside the surgery with half a dozen others, all shot in so many ways, blood running everywhere." James stopped as he saw the alarm in the ladies' eyes. "I'm sorry, but you see, it's like that, war, it's terrible. And our ships, being of wood, the spray of splinters does something terrible to you, tearing off the skin, and knocking you about."

"And you've had your share of splinters, I suppose?" added William.

"Oh yes, Mr. Garrett sir, that I have." James grinned sheepishly, and went on, "Well, I was trying not to listen to the screams that came from behind the surgery door — not hard with the noise of our cannon, and the French right up against us, that did us a service by muffling those poor wretches who were on their way to heaven, and of course, it was hard to see, all at night, with all the powder and smoke..."

The two women were spellbound and William stared fixedly at the floor, pausing every so often to take a meditative puff. Was he thinking of the same sort of scenes at his own past battles, James wondered. Is my story bringing back images he would rather forget? "Anyway, I hurried into the surgery. 'Beg pardon, sir, we have a man who —'

"'I know, I know, I have seven waiting, and more every minute,' the surgeon told me. 'I'm doing my best. Here, cut this sheet into four, give it back to me, see if you can take one and use it as a tourniquet. Then you'll have to cauterize him. I'll supervise.'

"I cut it as hastily as I could and hurried out. But as I kneeled beside him..." James paused his narration for a long moment, staring into space as though he were seeing the vision right here and now. "Poor fellow, he had gone." He nodded. "I made a sign of the cross over him, mumbled a prayer, and tore up the stairway back to my crew, where I took the dead man's place, thrusting the ramrod very inexpertly, I'm afraid, into the barrel.

"'Atta boy, sir, 'at does it!' my head gunner roared over the cannons' pounding.

"We stepped back and covered our ears, as it blasted yet another thirty-four pounder straight into the side of the *l'Orient*. 'Better look to yourself, sir!' He pointed.

"Blood was running down my leg. A splinter, well, yes, a sizeable chunk of wood, had lodged in my thigh. I plucked it out, tried to affix the flap of flesh shut, pressing it hard for a few seconds, and then went on firing."

"So the sight of blood is no stranger to ye, neither," said William.

"Oh no, I'm very much used to that. But hopefully, those days are gone forever. And soon, that slaughter will be forgotten in the good life here." But something compelled him to go on, almost as a memoriam to his friend. "You see, that gunner was the sly one, winking, and coming as close to insubordination as he could, with his wisecracks and knavish jokes. He was clever, hailed from Devon in fact, spoke with a thick accent. I always felt he should have been a Londoner, he'd probably have prospered there, rather than having been unfortunate enough to be press-ganged into service."

"Pressed?" Catherine asked.

"Yes, Catherine," he finally raised eyes, and took her

in with almost a shock, how lovely she looked with the firelight on her cheeks. "Well you see, they'd send crews out into the countryside — those in London being much too clever — to catch poor unsuspecting villagers, slip them the king's shilling, and once impounded, they'd grab 'em and get 'em on board."

"And they can't get off?"

"Well, I won't say never. But it is, as you may have heard, virtually impossible to escape from one of His Majesty's ships."

"You did!" blurted Catherine

James turned and looked at her. "Yes, I did. But I want you to know, Catherine, that I have been exonerated."

"Have you now?" broke in her mother.

"Aye, madam, that I have."

"When?" Catherine asked, her blue eyes watching his every reaction.

"Not too long ago..."

"After your visit here two years ago?"

"Oh yes..." James began to change the conversation away but was brought back abruptly by William.

"Now there's a tale worth telling..." William prompted.

A tale worth telling indeed. But James was not so sure he wanted to tell it. He was too afraid of the tears that might start into his eyes.

Chapter Twelve

James found it hard to know whether William Garrett was testing him or not. But he'd decided to make sure there'd be no more ghastly mistakes, no more brothers or townspeople running to JPs to thrust him into court all over again. If he told them now, though, it might be all over town later; it could mean he'd be accepted without any misunderstandings, such as some aberrant naval ship trying to do its duty by flogging him to death.

"Well, when I first arrived, it was utter wilderness, and I was rescued by a Micmac band, who were very good to me..." He paused, caught by the loneliness that rose to confront him, like a malignant spectre, every time the band was mentioned. "They saved my life, in fact, one winter. And, um..." he cleared his throat. "Well, a year later, their Chief fell ill, and they asked me to help. I soon saw that he needed an operation. No surgeons in New Carlisle for sure, but I'd seen our ship's surgeon work miracles on occasion, and so I decided I'd have to bring him to my ship."

"The *Billy Ruffian*?" gasped Catherine.

"Yes. You see, it was in port here, and no doctor in Paspébiac. So... well, finally Dr. Bellamy operated and, as I suspected, he was able to save the Chief's life. And by the way, that's how I came to be given the fine canoe, moored as it is now down at our breakwater! The band gave it to me as a present."

"But how did you get exonerated, laddie?" asked William gently.

"Well, you see, the penalty for desertion..."

"They do punish you, then?" asked Eleanor.

"They do, ma'am, and it's rather severe."

"What do they do?" burst out Catherine.

James held back. He was not sure that the company assembled by the open fire would like such extremes, nor did he wish here to denigrate his Navy. But they were all looking at him in keen anticipation.

"Well," he finally went on, "it's a thousand lashes, one hundred on each ship of the line."

The two women gasped, and William coughed mightily.

"How horrible!" Catherine exclaimed.

"What a dreadful and very long-drawn-out punishment."

"Not so drawn out, ma'am. You don't last beyond, well, the first ship, or if you're lucky, beyond half of that even. You certainly don't live to see the other nine."

"And they still keep doing it?"

"Aye. Just as long as there is anything left to lash, I suppose."

"How awfully horrid!" Mrs. Garrett raised a handkerchief to her eyes. "I had no idea." Catherine buried her face in her hands.

"You mean those rascal sons of yours would have subjected young James to that?" Eleanor looked at William in shock and anger.

"Now luv, they're your sons too, and they just got into some rum, and you know well, I punished them right and proper, I did. Y'see," he turned to James, "they were only going to turn you in as a sort of prank. Thank heaven we found out in time."

"You didn't find out in time, Papa," Catherine burst out, nearly in tears, "it was just that —," she stopped, "just that James was called away in time — before anything could happen." James could see she was not about to reveal that it was her own quick thinking that had saved his life.

"Well, anyway," William went on, sitting back in his chair and letting out a big puff of smoke, "you are exonerated now?"

"It appears so."

"You still didn't tell us how," William asked.

"Oh. Well, I didn't mean it to happen. It just... Somehow..." He was loath to give away the full details.

"Come on, out with it," William nudged. Perhaps he was beginning to believe it never happened.

"Well, you see, I knew that sending the Chief by himself with his canoes — well, you can imagine how they would treat a Native turning up in a Micmac canoe to a ship of the line of His Majesty. So I had to go along with him. You know, to make sure they did what was right and proper." James shrugged. "And that meant, of course..."

"They caught you!"

"Yes. They had me."

"Your life? You would have given up your life. To save another man? To save an Indian?" William took his pipe out of his mouth, staggered beyond belief.

"He was the Chief. He was my friend, sir. I had no other alternative, now did I? You know how it is..." James finished rather lamely. He stared at the floor.

William got to his feet as quickly as he could with his bum leg. "James, my man, I am honoured, yes indeed, honoured to come and shake your hand. What a fine specimen. I have seldom met, even in the depths of the Revolutionary War, anyone as brave as this sailor before me." He stood and surveyed the group. "You know, Hall's been telling me what you have been going through, back at the mill."

"The mill? Oh, I've been enjoying it, sir. Mr. Hall is a wonderful employer."

"Aye, that he is. But you're not getting my meaning, lad."

"Your meaning, sir?"

"Aye. He told me he's been watching you. He hinted to me, that he did, that this daughter of mine, here, takes up a lot of your thinking."

James raised his head, a frown creasing his brow. What was going on? Then he remembered voicing his feelings the night they had stitched the pulleys. After spending the afternoon with her, he'd been overcome with her presence, with desire. Had he said too much? Should he have kept quiet? He'd never suspected his views might be passed on. But of course, Hall and Garrett were partners. When they met, Hall would love to bring it up, especially with his distaste for the Brothertons. Well, what's done is done, he thought, and glanced at the young woman who was the object of this conversation. Her head was bowed, but one hand tightly clutched and twisted a portion of her skirt.

"Now Eleanor," William Sr. went on, "I know what you think of the Brothertons. And you know I don't much agree with that liking of yours. But after you've heard from our young visitor here, and how he put loyalty and friendship above all else, I know you agree with me that if he still wants the hand of our daughter in marriage, he can bloody well have it! And I hope, luv, you'd consider it as I do, a right honour for the whole family."

James looked up sharply. This is not at all what he had expected.

Catherine leapt up, grabbed her father, flung her arms around him, and kissed him hard.

James rose too, as Eleanor came to hug him. He could hardly restrain the tears of joy that leapt into his eyes. A new chapter in his life had certainly begun.

Chapter Thirteen

The next Sunday, his heart beating furiously, James beached the canoe at the foot of Shigawake brook. In the prow ahead, Catherine Garrett stepped out into the waves, soaking her skirt and shoes without care — she was anxious too, he saw, as little Ben leapt out with her and the two of them hauled the canoe in to shore. The only way old Will had permitted his daughter to go off with James alone was with a chaperone, and they had finally persuaded him that Ben fit the bill.

Ben was going back to work at the mill on Monday as Hall had requested, but James would only return for one week, depending of course on the outcome of Catherine's decision today. How well he knew that here, in this harsh land, women had to be practical, however much they loved a man. Would she approve of his cabin, albeit as temporary living quarters? Would she be brave enough to face the winter here, far from her family, in conditions fit for none but the hardiest? And all for a love which had not really been tested? Was James asking too much? Definitely, too much, he realized. Well, here they were, and go through with it he must.

He stepped out and helped them lift the canoe up above the high-tide line next to his brook that was tumbling down wide, red stone steps.

Catherine took up her own bag easily and slung it over her shoulder. "So this is the famous brook?"

"Aye. You like it?"

"'Tis pretty, James."

First hurdle crossed, he said to himself, and set off in the lead.

They headed up the trail, clearly marked but not well worn, between the brook and the steep sides of the Hollow. Home again after two long months: but happiness mingled with anxiety as this one day's expedition would decide whether she'd agree to become his wife.

So much hung in the balance. Deliberately he had refrained from telling her too many things about this "home", because every time he spoke, his eyes would glow and feelings spill out — one certain way to destroy any surprise or appreciation. How could he prevent her from being disappointed, today of all days? Nothing for it but let the site speak for itself. And of course, pray hard.

James waved to his left, where through the bare autumn trees could be seen a brow of flat land above. "As I told you, I intend to build a house further up there, and I've got the foundations more or less placed." He tried sounding optimistic, but saw how vapid that sounded — just foundations? "But the cabin is more or less fixed up, though." He heard anxiety ring in his voice.

"I have always wanted to sleep in the wild." Catherine sped up and passed him, as though more anxious than he, or was it more enthusiastic? "I remember when I was seven, Papa took me back to a neighbour's hunting cabin in the woods. Frightfully exciting, for someone my age."

She's just trying to put me at ease, James thought to

himself as he followed her. Well, heaven knows, I need it. I don't think I've been this anxious since the night I jumped off the *Billy Ruffian*. Was that only two years ago?

How much he had achieved! That first summer, with the help of his Micmac friends, he had found this brook and established his cabin. Then in the winter, he'd lived back in the interior with the Micmac, learning how to survive, trap small game, and other rules about surviving the extreme cold of the Gaspé Coast. The next summer in Paspébiac he'd learned a trade, caulking a ship's hull for Robin's, and last winter he'd worked in the woods for the Robin's Company. This summer he'd spent alone, working on his cabin, trying to fend off his depression from losing Magwés.

He watched Catherine, striding gamely along ahead, taking in everything so boldly. "It's so very wild," she commented. "We must be miles from anyone."

"Yes, miles," he replied, pleased at the thought.

"I suppose you get used to that?"

"I certainly hope so. But you know, Catherine," he said reassuringly, "it won't be long before neighbours appear. It's too good here. The land is rich and flat above, the trees tall and straight, just made for the walls of houses. It won't be long before this becomes as populated as New Carlisle."

She laughed.

"All right then," he said, "perhaps not like New Carlisle, but certainly I predict that one day there will be a string of homes all the way along the shore, from here to Paspébiac."

"I wonder if we will ever live to see that?"

"Well, if we never see it, I shall be just as happy." The sides of the Hollow, as James called it, became less prominent as the valley floor broadened into a flat and arable, though swamplike, land. So far so good, perhaps, but what on earth would she think when they actually came upon his meagre cabin, which now he saw through her eyes as very rough, indeed even primitive and uncomfortable? What had he got himself into? He should never have agreed to this. He'd lose her forever, he knew. Or else she'd insist upon them living in New Carlisle, with neighbours like Billy Brotherton.

Well, be prepared, he told himself. He could see even more clearly how no woman in her right mind would ever stick it out under these circumstances. And the closer they came to his cabin, the more nervous he got, the more torn, and the more he kicked himself for having been fool enough to allow this test in the first place.

"I do love you, James," she had protested one night. "I'll follow you anywhere." He had been holding her in his arms for a brief moment when saying good-bye outside the door as he left for his week at the mill.

But this early morning as she had prepared for the canoe trip, he could see that resolve weakening. Her brothers, he guessed, had been working on her, especially Will, who for some reason seemed to have taken a dislike to him. Forget Billy Brotherton, tons of young men in New Carlisle would love to wed and bed her. She must know all that, he said to himself. Why wouldn't she be leery? His nervousness rose exponentially.

"Wait, before we see the cabin, shall we rather look at what you intend to build?"

"You mean, go back up to the site of our future house?"

"Yes, is it so far?"

Cold feet, that's what she had, he thought. But what a letdown to see that clearing. "No, but it's a climb. Maybe we should wait until after you have seen the cabin."

"I just thought it might be an idea to go there first."

"Well, I've only got a few foundations placed," he began, "and I'm not sure that —"

She stopped and looked at him. "James, I would like to see that first." Yes, this was an important moment in her life, too. He'd been so centred on himself, on his own nervousness, he'd been ignoring the fact that she would be leaving house and home to come and live with him, and she was taking all this seriously. Almost too seriously. But then again, wasn't it a serious decision?

"All right. There's a pathway just ahead, the one I use going up from the cabin to the site. Follow me."

James led the way up the path and then at the top, he stopped. Pretty well a disaster! Cut trees lay topsy-turvy, waiting for some future ox to sled them over to the rough foundations. Broken bushes and saplings littered the clearing. The open space itself was so small, you could never imagine the hard work he'd done to get it this far.

Saying nothing, he forged on, leading Catherine and Ben through untamed underbrush. He stopped at the straight line of rocks he had brought from the beach. Each one had been such a struggle, and now they lay, hidden among shrubbery. Pretty sad.

"The bay!" Catherine exclaimed. "It does look wonderful from here."

A rescue, sort of. "That was my idea." James gladly seized upon the notion. "And see, up behind? That hill will shield us from the north wind." He loosed his imagination: "I can just see us on the veranda, rocking, bringing up the children, looking out at the bay."

"James," Ben now stood beside them, "I'd say rockin' on some veranda looks to me a long ways off."

"I guess so. But how did everyone else's house get built?"

"With help," Catherine said firmly, "lots of help." She looked determined, "I'll see to that."

"So you like the site?"

"I like the view," she relied enigmatically. "Now I'll visit the famous cabin."

Oh-oh, even Ben looked despondent, James thought. His heart sank, but he tried to make light of it all, knowing he was fighting a losing battle.

Finally, the little party of three wound around a turn in the brook and came to the bridge James had built two years before. He paused, staring at the water flecked with sunshine, which had pierced the tree cover. Such a comforting sound. He had forgotten how delightful his brook sounded.

"What are we waiting for?" asked Catherine.

"Almost there," James tried to sound reassuring.

"Pretty wild here, James," Ben called. "Ain't you afraid to live here all by yer lonesome?"

"Not at all, Ben," James replied. "You have the sound of the brook for company, 'tis a real comfort, I can tell you."

"Not when a bear comes up!"

"Oh, I've seen bears all right, and one time —" he stopped himself. That would just frighten Catherine. For he had nearly been killed in one encounter right here.

"You built it all by yourself?"

"I did." And all too soon, they came to the edge of the clearing.

James stopped. Catherine stepped up beside him, Ben third. They stood.

James shut his eyes. He couldn't even bear to look at Catherine. The moment had come. Or had it?

"This your cabin?"

"It is, Ben. Do you like it?"

"Terble nice fer maybe a few days. Never live here meself, though. I'd be much too scared."

Still Catherine hadn't spoken.

"Thanks for the encouragement, Ben," James heard himself retort. "We are trying to impress Catherine, remember?"

Catherine grabbed his hand, and he turned to look at her. She was smiling.

He turned to look at it again, trying to see it through her eyes. "Well?"

"Well... the outside is... not what I expected exactly. But..." She paused.

His heart pounded and then, as the saying goes, leapt into his mouth. "I think..." she went on. "I think..."

"Yes?" Lost forever, no doubt, he said to himself. Well, learn to live with it.

"May we look inside?"

"Of course, of course. Come." They started forward. "You see, Catherine —" he stopped himself. Don't be pessimistic, he reprimanded himself.

Before opening the door, James paused once more to offer up a prayer. He turned and saw Ben watching cautiously. But the lad did seem a little more pleased. Taking heart, James swung the cabin door ajar. Catherine stepped in.

Ben followed.

James waited. "It's very rough," he began, "and it's not finished. There's so much I intend to do, you know, I'm going to get us a better table, not hard to build, and I'll be —"

She turned and put her fingers on his lips, to silence him. Then having taken in the interior, she moved around, studying each item carefully, stepping over to the open fireplace, kneeling and feeling the smooth stones blackened by fires, while his tension mounted. Worse than facing that bear, he said to himself. "You know," he went on anxiously, "I've been working outside, but I promise —"

"James, don't apologize." Catherine rose from the fireplace and went on to examine the shelving.

James closed his eyes.

"It's amazing, one fella did this all by himself!" Ben went to sit on the bed frame.

Catherine came over to James and waited until he opened his eyes again. So much hung on her reply.

"We'll make this work," she said. "It's a great challenge, but I will do my best."

"You will?"

"Of course. We shall be very happy here, James. It's not exactly what I expected. But perhaps... it's even better." She went to the door, and looked out. "You own all this land around here? It's all yours?"

He nodded. "Looks like it."

"You mean, you don't have any title?"

"No, of course not. But we can claim land we build on. Especially in waste lands of the Crown."

"I hope so," she murmured.

"So now, Catherine, you've seen it all. Well, not all. The land behind stretches a long way, and out along the cliffs too. Enough for generations of children to farm. Lots of acres for wheat and barley, and flax, and oats for the horses and hay for the oxen. We can expand here as much as we like."

"Until those droves of settlers you talk about find out, and come to drive us out," she said, allowing a little smile to cross her face. Was she teasing him?

"You're right," he said. "Well, maybe we should go back to New Carlisle. You can decide later, Catherine. I'm ready for anything. And perhaps one day..."

"One day, yes..." She paused. James looked at his feet. "And that day is today, James. I have decided, my love." She reached out and took his hand. "James, you're giving me what I always wanted, a home of my own." He looked at her. "I've played second fiddle to my brothers for so long, and had to obey Father and Mother who don't always make things easy. Now there is just you and me. No bride will ever have a better home than this one right here. It's perfect. And whatever is not perfect, we'll make it so. Together."

Chapter Fourteen

Dear Mother,

I write to you this morning as a newly married man. There has not been one morning this summer that I have not awakened and told myself — today I will write to my dearest Mother. But so many events in this New World have conspired against my having the time to sit and compose a proper letter.

First, my new wife. Her name is Catherine Garrett, and she is all that I have ever hoped. In fact, she appears much as you must have looked at her age. Blonde, blue eyes, with her robust body she can be a real worker. Why the Lord above blessed me with such a gracious and hard-working partner, I have no idea. But I offer thanks daily, as you must know.

Secondly, His help brought me to a part of the wilderness with a vigorous stream running through, and lots of timber to build our own house — I have already made a small cabin. No neighbours for miles around. I know what you are thinking — how will Catherine like that? Well, in spite of the great risks involved, I brought her to see it before we wed. She approved. And thither we go this week to set up life together.

Through a stroke of good fortune, my Micmac friends (the Indians hereabouts who rescued me) gave me a birchbark canoe. So we shall canoe down from New Carlisle, the Loy-alist village on the Gaspé coast, to my little brook, which the Micmac call Shegouac.

I have spoken to Catherine about you, dear Mother, and it is our combined plan to bring you across the sea to join us, if you would like. This promise I shall be in a position to keep next year, once Catherine and I have our little habitation built and in a presentable shape. Think about it, dear Mother, but not too hard, because things often take time in this New World. It would be a life of hardship, no doubt, but one of complete freedom. You will go where you like and do what you want. Although of course, we work from dawn to dusk, planting, cutting trees and making a farm out of what, so far, are desperately thick woods, rocks, and other impediments to any hopes of a leisurely life.

Please write care of William Garrett, my father-in-law, at New Carlisle, in the province of Lower Canada. This letter may take a long time to reach you but I am hoping to send it on a schooner direct to England in the hopes it will find you somehow at Raby Castle. When you have a moment, please write back to me about your present state, and your future intentions. I do of course hope this finds you well and happy, as I have no cause to believe otherwise.

Your loving son, ever,

James Alford

PS. You should know that because I was pursued as a de-serter, I had to change my name. So please write to me as James Alford.

James sat back and looked down at the parchment. Al-ready the sun had risen to shaft in the side window. It was Sunday morning; the wedding party the night before had been long and full of cheer — rum, good food, dancing, and now the entire family was asleep upstairs.

Although it had been their wedding night, both he and Catherine had slept here by the fire, his bed over the past two weeks. With little Eleanor sharing her room, Catherine preferred to use this room downstairs for the few nights remaining before they struck out to their own place.

His body still felt that beautiful relaxation, drained by love-making. He looked across at Catherine, still deeply asleep, a flush of passion upon her cheeks, her blonde hair awry, her nightgown beside her in a tangled heap. He got up, quietly tiptoed over, and tucked it under the covering. She did not stir.

He straightened and looked upstairs. How would she dress when the brothers came down, he wondered in an unusual proprietary fashion. Just as he was thinking this, he heard the boards creak above. Mrs. Garrett always came down first, to feed the fire and prepare a kettle for their tea and a cauldron for their porridge. Well, here comes breakfast. But his main thought was now, as it had been all along: how to tell his new wife of the journey he planned to see his son and the Micmac tribe?

***

"Mrs. James Alford..." Catherine was saying. She had a lovely red plaid shawl over her shoulders, one of the better wedding presents that they had received.

James was inordinately proud of his new wife as they took their walk down to the pier. The late October weather had turned cold, giving rise to a much earlier blaze of glory that covered the Gaspé coast every autumn. These last days working in Will Garrett's fields, James had marvelled, as he did every year since coming to the New World, at the lime greens and reds, dark greens, lemon yellows, bright and dark, of the many trees surrounding William Garrett's farm. The trees seemed to reflect his spirit, which soared like the colours of the landscape. A time of festivity, of rejoicing, a conflagration of yearning and satisfaction. So how would he break the news to her of his impending journey?

"You know, I have been Catherine Garrett for nineteen years..."

"Well, you will be Catherine Alford for nineteen plus nineteen plus another nineteen," he said. "And I shall love you for twice as long as that."

They walked a little further and stopped to survey the open common fields with their cattle and sheep. "So what is it you wanted to discuss with me, my dearest?" Catherine asked, reaching for his hand.

How shall I bring it up, he wondered again. "Catherine, I want to make a short trip by canoe down the coast to make sure everything is fine before you come. I will be gone only two days."

"A wife's duty is to be by her husband. I cannot let you go alone."

Exactly the answer he had anticipated. Did that mean he would have to tell her the whole truth? One day after their wedding? "No, my love. Absolutely not. I intend to go alone. Any storm may surprise me, and I would rather take as much of our supplies as possible down to our cabin in advance. I need the room in the canoe."

"But I can learn to paddle, James. I have to start soon, as you yourself acknowledged."

"We'll have lots of time for that," James replied.

He saw Catherine look sideways at him. "I think you're hiding something."

Would he have rather had a less discerning wife? One with less intuition? Someone less intelligent perhaps? No siree! He loved her for that very perception. "You are just wonderful, Catherine!"

She said nothing, but withdrew her hand from his.

"It will only be for two days," James said. "I'll be back on the evening of the second day, no matter what."

"No matter if there is that storm you predict?"

"Well then, I shall come one day later. I have every reason to preserve my life, now that it seems so promising."

"I can't believe we're disagreeing this soon after our wedding," Catherine said with a hint of anger.

"No argument at all," retorted James. "A husband has an obligation to prepare his house for his bride, and nothing you say will dissuade me. You think I have another wench hidden in the woods?"

"You have something hidden in the woods," she said. "Of that I am sure."

They kept walking toward the jetty without speaking. They reached it and stood out upon the floating boards, listening to the waters lap around them. The sky was half covered in lush clouds, different shades of a gentle blue-grey. To the right, white flecks and buffets crossed at different levels, some high, some low, exemplifying the immense variety of a Gaspé sky — wrought by a Master to whom James felt very close.

James wanted so much to resolve this amicably, but he could see no other way: the truth must not come now, it must wait till later. How much later, he did not know. "I shall leave tomorrow morning, Catherine, and let's not find ourselves divided over so small a trifle as two days." He looked across at her.

She did not return his look, but instead, sat on the piling. Then she stooped and reached her white arm down into the blue waters of the bay and dabbled her fingers in the wavelets.

What a lovely sight! I shall be so glad, he decided, when this whole difficult past is out in the open. The time will come, soon enough, when I'm forced to reveal everything.

They stood there on the jetty, looking out at two schooners and a barque moored close to the lee of land, rocking at anchor, and several fishing boats. All seemed calm, with the glorious Gaspé cloud patterns high above, but unnoticed now by the young couple struggling with their mounting difficulties.

Chapter Fifteen

The sun was setting behind James as he drove the canoe through the waves toward Port Daniel. This morning, he had brought most of the supplies for the long autumn ahead and first beached the canoe at his brook. Making several trips to the cabin on the run, he wasted not a second, hastily arranging the wedding presents, the flour, sugar, molasses, and other foodstuffs they had been given. They had even received tea, a costly gift, more valuable than the rum for a time of celebration. Then he had raced back to the canoe, jumped in, and pushed off eastward toward his Micmac tribe.

After his walk with Catherine yesterday, festivities had continued at the Garretts', for relatives had come from Gaspé to join them. Catherine seemed to have forgotten her earlier irritation — or was it anger? That night, lying with her by the fire, he had made a few gentle overtures, but she had rolled on her side to look at him.

"I'm sorry, Catherine," he had whispered, "I'm so sorry. I had no intention of upsetting you. But this stubbornness of mine, 'tis a trait for which I have often been chastised. I must try to rid myself of it. You will have to help me, for I have long been known for... um... well, willful obstinacy."

She studied him, looking deep into his eyes, illuminated as she was by a faint glow from the dying embers.

The candles had been blown out for they were costly to buy and arduous to make, and whale oil for the two lamps the Garretts owned had risen in price. "I want you to know, James, that I trust you. And I know that whatever secret it is —"

"Secret, my love? What are you —?"

"Ssh!" She put her fingers on his lips. "Do not incriminate yourself with a lie," she said, "just listen. I know you're hiding something. And I know, equally well, my dear James, that you will tell me all in good time. I trust in the Lord. And He tells me that you will do what is required. So I shall remain a dutiful and faithful wife, until that time."

***

James rounded Port Daniel point which was a good hard afternoon's paddle from Shigawake brook. He headed into the very estuary where his ship, the *Bellerophon*, had moored two years before during a storm. The experience washed over him once again: the angry waves bashing the ship's hull, his dangerous swim, arriving safely by the grace of God, and then making his way up the river until the Micmac had captured him.

Paddling toward Port Daniel, he remembered his first view of Little Birch, kneeling beside him as he recovered in her warm wigwam; her almond eyes, dark and piercing, her smooth skin, her silky, black hair; and then the two of them with fascination and love watching the Northern Lights that long cold winter he had spent with her family in the interior plateau. Then — how well he saw it! — that moment when, in Micmac tradition, he had proposed to her by tossing the smooth pebble from the river's bed into her lap. She had picked it up and with long slim fingers pressed it to her lips, signifying she would accept him as her husband for life. He could not stop the tears rising and at long last allowed himself to cry. Shoulders hunched and head bowed, he bawled like the baby he was going to see, his only son, John. He had never cried for John and for the death in childbirth of his wife Little Birch. The grief then had floored him for days, if not weeks, when he had lain in her family's wigwam, refusing all food and succour. He now realized that even when he had revived, thanks to the ministrations of their shaman, the *Buowin,* he had not cried even then. About time now to give in to the tears so long repressed, out here alone in his fine canoe. And so he floated on the wide estuary, broken and lost.

The day was chill, damp, the cold came in billows which sped double layered clouds over his head. The canoe swayed in a gentle rocking that soothed him.

After a time, he picked up the paddle and as tears kept running down his face, he stroked the canoe toward the narrow opening of the river.

He allowed himself a glance at the trading post, whose men had tried to track and capture him for the Navy. He saw two figures on the wood stoop of the distant post, watching. One, he felt sure, would be the trader. At this distance, they might make sense of his Micmac jacket, but his hair had been shortened, his face clean shaven, so he wasn't sure how he'd be regarded. Then, his anger rose. His knife hung, in the fashion of the Micmac, round his neck; he'd not hesitate to use it should those men come after him.

He switched his attention to the narrow, rushing river mouth. Navigate that first, worry about any attack later. The canoe, empty save for a few presents he had brought, rode too high for this turbulence. So he nosed up the centre, driving with all his might. The canoe bobbed and twisted as he mounted the churning waters. Don't let up! Panting, he stroked harder and further until he reached the placid lagoon behind the Port Daniel sandbank.

Had the two men come after him? They were obscured now by the trees. No sign of pursuit. Good. Had they taken him for just another Micmac? Still apprehensive, his swift strokes drove him over the calm surface toward clumps of pine, birch, and spruce hugging the entrance to the upper river.

Would the band welcome him? Was his son happy? Had he grown? A newborn when James had left in June, he'd be five months old. Be wary, be on guard for Fury, the villainous Micmac who had wanted him killed. Try to behave just like one of the band.

Yes, he did feel like one of the band, no doubt — closer to them than to the settlers in New Carlisle. And he let his strokes lengthen, assume an easier rhythm, as he headed up toward the Micmac mooring.

***

Leaving the canoe behind, he trotted up the trail, watching for the trip-line that warned the band someone approached. It had caught him once before and sent him flat. He saw it ahead and leaped over. Surprise them, he thought.

And surprise them he did. He reached the scattering of birchbark wigwams under the trees that he remembered so well. Three or four children recognized him and ran over, calling excitedly to their parents, surrounding him. Rejoicing, he picked some up and laughed as he made his way toward the wigwam of Full Moon, his former mother-in-law.

Having heard the commotion, she emerged from her birchbark dwelling. When she saw him, she brightened and called inside. A younger woman appeared in the low opening, took one look, and dove back. He embraced Full Moon warmly, forgetting that this was not in their tradition, apologizing as she shrank a little. The other woman, only a teenager, emerged and held out the baby, now almost six months old.

His young son, John.

He took up John, strapped as he was to a *keenakun*, the Micmac cradle board, and held him high. Then he crushed him to himself as though this were life itself.

John began to scream. "I'm sorry, John, I'm sorry. Here." James handed his son back to the young woman.

"She is our *nùjiakunùsa*. She has saved his life," Full Moon told him in Micmac.

James was puzzled at the word. Did it mean, a wet-nurse? He wondered where Tongue could be, the band's translator.

He had not long to wait. The burly Indian soon arrived, with several others gathering round. He greeted James warmly and led him to the Chief's wigwam for the ritual welcome.

Once inside, James was surprised at how comfortable it all felt. Little was said: the encounter had none of the excited chatter that would mark any European reunion. He solemnly handed the Chief, who emanated warmth, his present of tobacco. Then James stuffed the ceremonial pipe, placed a glowing brand against its bowl, and inhaled. Tongue, who had entered to translate, could not avoid reminding James of the first time he had smoked in here: how he had coughed and sputtered. All three broke out laughing again.

"Don't worry, I'll probably do it again." James drew in a mouthful of smoke as the Chief and Tongue watched expectantly. He blew it out without coughing, pleased with himself. They nodded assent.

After the ritual welcome in which Tongue acted as a mediator, James and the Chief exchanged news. James expressed his gratitude again for the present of the superb canoe. Pausing for Tongue to translate, he told how easy the trip had been for him now between New Carlisle and Shegouac, where he intended to live. For the moment, James thought it better not to mention his marriage to Catherine.

Afterwards, James went across in the deepening dusk to Full Moon's wigwam where her brother, One Arm, and her son, Brightstar, were sitting around the fire. As the wet-nurse was preparing an evening meal, James was introduced to her young husband, scarcely out of his teens himself.

With Tongue there, they could exchange news and stories of the baby, his doings, how he had even now started to crawl. The first thing James did was to give a nickname to the young woman who had been acting as a wet-nurse to John.

"I shall call you Sunrise," he said in Micmac, "because

you have given my son a new day." Brightstar, the twelve-year-old brother of Little Birch, clapped his hands in delight. The others giggled, and Sunrise did seem pleased. How young she looked, even though all the Native women appeared younger than their years. She was short and stocky, but with ample breasts for milk and a sunny smile. She seemed to enjoy her position with her new family, especially now that the long-awaited father of the child had returned.

John was soon unlaced and allowed to crawl around on a blanket, and crawl he did. Full Moon went on to explain that John spent his day, as did every Micmac child, wrapped in soft beaverskin and safely strapped onto the flat board. A hoop of ash curved over his head as protection. Thus the baby could be taken everywhere, leaned up against a tree, or in cases of danger hung from a high limb. Worn on the back with a tump line around the forehead, the board's ample width protected the baby from limbs of branches while the mother made her way through thick woods. James noticed several little toys hung from the curved hoop. One particularly attracted James, and he fingered it. The toy hung on a thread, a dogwood loop strung with a web of vegetable fibres.

"Not toy — protection!" One Arm told him. "Trap for evil spirits which come take baby's spirit. Baby's spirit weak, easy to be snatched. Many infants get sick and die." The spider spirits had taught the Micmac how to make these, and in fact, how to make nets for fish too. "Spider spirits very good spirits," One Arm concluded.

James felt happy and relieved they were taking such good care of his son. And only too soon, the pointed question arrived: Would he be coming back to live with the band?

No, sadly, he had to leave first thing in the morning. But he would come back often and eventually might collect his son and bring him back into his own world, to live in his cabin or the larger farmhouse he hoped to build.

This announcement did not fall happily upon his beholders. Take the child from the tribe? What could he be thinking, they asked. Where was the woman, the mother, that every child needed? What about brothers and sisters and other children to play with?

For his part, James was concerned about John during this next winter. What would the band do? How would Full Moon and One Arm survive? One Arm told him they would hunt again as always back on the plateau of the caribou. The Chief had adopted this family for now, and would look after them in his own enclave. After all, he had said, did not the Chief owe his life to James?

"And how did they find you, Sunrise?" James asked in Micmac, stalling for time so he could think about their apparent refusal to give up his son.

She hailed from Listiguj, the main community of Micmac up at the mouth of the Matapedia River where Chaleur Bay began. But she and her young husband had been fishing with a group on the Gesgapegiag River, a salmon river on the far side of New Carlisle. The Micmac communities all along the shore were in constant touch. The disaster of Little Birch's death had been passed on at once, and Sunrise had canoed swiftly up to the Port Daniel band to feed and nourish the new, motherless baby. She had lost her own baby the week before, and now she and her husband would join the Chief's enclave back in caribou country until the next spring, when she could go back to her Listiguj band and presumably start her own family over again.

Thus reassured that his son was well cared for, with good plans laid for the winter, James decided he could leave the next morning for New Carlisle, happy. He was intensely worried about how John and he would be reunited. And how he should tell Catherine. Certainly not before they could provide good provisions over the long winter, perhaps a couple of years or more. He had told Full Moon he was "looking for a suitable mother for John." But had that fallen on deaf ears?

Catherine, with her fiery spirit, would be his main obstacle. Better wait until they had a child of their own, he decided. But then again, would that not make it even harder? Difficult times ahead.

Chapter Sixteen

The cry of the water-driven saw winding down still gave James an uncomfortable feeling in the pit of his stomach. He could not for the life of him forget the image of Ben's blood spurting into the air. But he hurried on down the roadway toward the sound, worried about Ben, and also the lumber Hall owed him for his weeks of work. He was not looking forward to this: Hall had been miffed at James for not helping at the mill this autumn, and had not even attended the wedding.

As the mill came into view, he headed down to find Ben hard at work, sporting the brace of leather round his neck that James had rigged to hold the handle of the wheelbarrow. James watched as Ben wheeled a load of sawdust over to a new white pile. "Ben!"

Ben dropped the wheelbarrow, unhooked his sling, and James gave him a hug as he might his own son. "Well Benigno, how is it all going along? The sling we made seems to be working."

"Oh yes, James," Ben said, "and Mr. Hall give me a raise!"

"Did he now? Wonderful news." Well, that took care of his first problem. But what about the approaching winter, when the mill stopped working? For himself, he was going to Shegouac with Catherine the next morning, and would stay by his brook, trapping, snaring, and fishing through the ice. "I wish I could bring you, Ben, but I don't know how we'll make it ourselves; these winters are long."

"You going up there to that wild place all by yourselves? You think that's best for the missus?"

James did have his doubts, for sure. "But it's you I'm worried about."

"Oh don't worry, I found me a good place this winter. I get to feed animals, and look for eggs — old Wida' Travers, her husband died last spring. She says she'll feed me all winter long. Her children is growed, and they promised to bring us food if we git into trouble. She told me she has three barrels of flour already. Should last us."

"Very good, Ben! The Lord does look after you. I hope you thank Him properly."

"I do, James. Every day. Specially fer giving me a friend like you."

James slapped his shoulder a couple of times, and then headed up the path to the wide entrance of the mill. Pleased at Hall's treatment of Ben, James shifted focus to his next problem, getting his lumber for his house next spring.

Mr. Hall looked up as he entered, and frowned, pointing to the saw. James saw that he did not have another assistant to run it so stood in wait, confined to his own thoughts.

His son, yes, he longed for his son, but he realized that he'd have a big problem getting him away from the tribe. He was even unsure how he and Catherine would survive this winter. Enough trout in the brook, maybe, but they would need more than that. On his recent stopover, he'd noticed little progress from the turnips and potatoes he'd planted among the stumps in the spring. Most of all, they would need a barrel of flour, which perhaps the Garretts might give them. He could possibly shoot a moose, depending on blizzards, ice storms, and other vagaries of a Gaspé winter. And how would they fare together in just one small room?

In due course Hall stopped the mill and walked over. "Come for your lumber?"

"I have that," James replied. "But I need nothing until the spring. The logs marked with Garretts' insignia are half mine, as my father-in-law and I have agreed."

Hall looked at him askance, and then the two of them went through the calculations they had agreed upon. James had counted on being able to draw upon some of the boards that Hall himself owned, as well as some of the Garretts' supply.

"And what d'ye intend to do with the fact that I trained ye for being a fine mill assistant and you're letting it all go to waste?"

"You don't think I gave as good as I got?" asked James.

"Not nearly," Hall replied. "You could get a job in any mill on the Coast now, with the training you got from me."

"The only mill I'd ever work for is yours." James looked the old man in the eye. "I was very happy working here and I know I could be so again. It's just that now I have got myself a wife. And well you know how I've longed to be a real settler with a real family. I've never lied to you on that point."

Hall met his gaze. "No, I'll grant ye that." Was he mollified?

"But I don't want to leave you in a state of dissatisfaction neither," James pressed. "Why don't you suggest what would be fair to deduct for my training? I'll gladly honour your proposal, Mr. Hall, if I can."

The old man grudgingly got out his pipe, and James watched once more in awe as he managed the tinderbox with deft fingers, getting his pipe alight in a trice.

It gave both of them time to think.

"Well, I'll allow as how ye did work hard, and you did save Ben's life. And you're an honourable man. And you served His Majesty well in the Royal Navy. Mr. Garrett's been telling me, and not only me but the whole village of New Carlisle, how his new son-in-law fought through the great naval battles on behalf of His Majesty. So maybe... maybe I'll give you all that we agreed on. Providing you honour your word to me that you'll not work at another mill. And that I can count on ye, if times get a bit hard up my way."

"I'll certainly do that, Mr. Hall," James said. "I certainly will." And he reached out his hand and the old fellow shook it.

***

Husband and wife should not keep anything from each other, James felt, and regretted keeping his former life a secret. But how should he bring it up? They had only been back on his land a short time. Already he had taught her where wild asparagus grew, and where to find fiddleheads and other edible wild plants. In spring, he would show her how to make maple syrup. Catherine had been impressed with his knowledge gained from the Micmac, and had not questioned him on that aspect. But was it bothering her? Something was definitely on her mind, he could see that. And he wondered how soon he should try and clear it all up.

With the leaves long fallen from the trees, James worked hard at clearing his land by the cliffs. He had just finished felling another tree when he saw Catherine's supple figure climbing up the trail from the Hollow.

He straightened. "Welcome sight!"

Catherine handed him a container of water. "I've already caught trout for our lunch, and found some roots for dinner. I also managed a new batch of loaves. So I thought I would come up to help you out."

"Gratefully received!" He drank thirstily from the container, which he had devised a while back, double-stitching the canvas seams of a piece of old sail, to make it waterproof.

Catherine set to work. "Welcome change from the cabin, being up here in the sun."

The blue sky above them, flecked only by whorls of cirrus, gave a warm autumn sun full access. No hint of a storm. They worked hard and silently, James felling another tree, and Catherine hauling the brush to a pile at one side.

"I brought up more beach stones for the foundations. See?"

"Hard work," Catherine commented.

"Gotta be done."

"Well, you know what we've discussed."

"An ox, I know, but how will we get one? No barn to keep it, no money to buy it, and anyway, who's got a spare calf to sell these days?" It did look impossible. And without an ox, all hope of making a farm was lost. He added brightly, "Well, it may all happen in good time."

"I'm sure. But you know," she stooped, picked up some branches, "chickens don't need much feed. And ducks. We could have fresh eggs. Then kill the chickens during the winter."

"Yes yes, good thought. Next trip to New Carlisle."

That night, at supper, James still avoided what was really on his mind, his child and his past. And before they had burned too much of their candle, they got into bed, worn out. But still entranced with the novelty of each other's bodies, they mostly made love. Afterwards, a deep sleep. Such a good life, he reflected. But unless he faced up to his secret past, this would not, could not, last.

Chapter Seventeen

"That brush pile we've been making, we'll burn it after there's snow on the ground," said James a few evenings later. "Maybe Christmas time. Make a nice bonfire in celebration."

Catherine paused as she was laying out their supper in the semi-dark of the cabin, the trees masking the dying light of the sun.

He caught her look. "Something on your mind, Catherine?"

"I have been giving this winter some serious thought, my dear." She reached out and touched his arm. "You seem to know so much about how to survive, I see that. Getting it all from those Micmac. But —"

So that was it, he thought. The Micmac. Had the time finally come? "Can you see all right?"

"Not really. But we don't have a lot of whale oil... Are you changing the subject?"

"Not at all." James went to the shelf, took down the lamp and placed it by them. Had he better start in? "Well, I do have some things I could go over..."

"Good." Although she had tried to make that sound casual, James knew a lot would hang on his reply.

He plucked a brand from the fire with tongs. "Well, I did live in the woods all one winter with a Micmac family." He held the brand to the wick, and watched until, after a few moments, it caught fire. "That's how I learned to snare small animals, how to trap, even how to shoot with a bow and arrow —"

"You told me all that, James. But you didn't tell me you lived with a family." He saw her studying his face.

"How about those trout?" he sat back, prevaricating.

Made motionless by his story, she recovered and began to dish up their meal. "Of course, sorry."

"It was the only way to survive. They were a wonderful family, in fact: the mother I called Full Moon, and her brother, One Arm."

"No husband?" Beside his four fried trout, she added a slab of cornmeal bread.

"Big Birch? Oh, he had died in a fishing accident. That's the reason I was there, because the brother, you see, had a withered arm, and couldn't really shoot with a bow and arrow. So the Chief asked me to go with them."

"Did you enjoy it?"

"Well, enjoy isn't really the word." James put the lamp on the rough table between them and sat to eat. "I learned a tremendous amount —"

"And so you and Full Moon... Her with no husband and you single..."

"No no, Catherine she had grown-up children. Don't jump to conclusions. Look, I did learn a lot from them all."

"All?"

"Oh yes, well there were Full Moon's two children." He paused, then eating slowly, went on. "They saved my life, in fact." James noticed her quickening interest but went on, "In fact, I was coming back from a trapline in early spring, and I went to cross a stream on an icy log, and slipped and fell in. It was hellish cold, I can tell you. I got soaked. Anyway, I just got out and kept walking. But soon I became so tired, probably chilled and frozen and not having eaten much, out on that trapline..." He paused again.

Catherine's eyes softened as she became caught up in the story.

"I wanted so much to lie down and just take a nap." He paused with a mouthful of trout. "Catherine if you ever get tired, you're freezing and it's midwinter, never, never give in to that fatigue. It really takes hold! You have to keep going." Getting involved in his story, and his food, he did not notice Catherine hanging on to every word.

"I would not be here if they hadn't found me — in fact, they got me back to their winter wigwam, covered me in blankets, and then Full Moon got in next to me on one side, and Little Birch on the other — naked, both of them, I found out later."

He glanced up to see Catherine trying to suppress her shock.

"Nothing untoward, of course," he went on hastily, "but their bodies warmed me. You have to understand, Catherine, that the only way to warm someone as cold as I was is exactly like that. It's well known by Eskimos, and the Micmac had gotten hold of it. Saved my life, really. Definitely. Saved my life. I shall be forever grateful to them."

"And who is Little Birch, my love?"

"Little Birch?" James looked up. It had come out so

naturally. But now, the awful moment was at hand. He chewed on another mouthful of trout.

"Yes, who is she? It is a simple enough question."

James stared into space. Well, he decided, speak up! "An Indian. She died." He stared into the glowing embers of the fire, overcome.

Had he looked sideways, he would have seen realization growing on the face of Catherine. "Go on, James, tell me."

He struggled with his emotions. "Well, Catherine, after the Chief had asked me to winter with them — you remember, I managed to get him to our ship's surgeon when he needed that operation. So they claim I saved his life." You're digressing, he told himself. "But that was afterwards."

"After what, James?" Catherine asked gently.

"After... after the winter."

"The winter? And presumably the spring? And presumably the summer..."

"Yes," James replied in a kind of trance, "after the summer." Then he cleared his throat and sat up straight, and turned to look at her.

She dropped her eyes, put her hands to her face. "All right, tell me everything, James. I'm ready."

He paused. "I was going to tell you sooner or later. It has nothing to do with us, Catherine. It all happened well before we got together. I suppose, after spending the winter with her, with Little Birch, with her family, in close proximity — there's nothing closer and more confining than a winter wigwam — I came to know her really well. She was such a fine person. I taught her to speak English, and she taught me to speak Micmac."

"I wondered how you spoke so well, James. I knew you would tell me." She dropped her hands, her shoulders slumped, her eyes bored into the embers of the fire. "Please go on."

"Well, what happened was..." He paused. Catherine stiffened, he saw. The longer he took, the worse it would be. Blurt it out! "Well, we got married in a kind of Micmac ceremony in the spring, and then we spent some time together."

"Where?"

"Where? Oh... Well, actually, there in the community, and... Well, here at this cabin and... But as I said, she died. I was devastated, dear Catherine, I do confess to that."

"I would hope so..."

Reassured, James allowed himself to go on. "I think I have never felt so badly, Catherine. I was in complete despair, I didn't eat and saw no one. And then their medicine man — they call him a *Buowin* — he came to my wigwam. He helped me come alive again. So then I came back here this spring, alone. All by myself. I worked hard. I planted corn. I tried sowing wheat. For over a month. But I just could not bear the loneliness, the unhappiness, even though I worked very hard to put this whole past out of my mind. It was only then I allowed myself to come to New Carlisle and find you. And that, I suppose, is why I did not come the previous summer."

"Because you were with her."

James nodded.

"You were with her. All that summer. While I was waiting for you..."

James nodded again, in despair.

All at once, Catherine allowed herself to give vent to suppressed emotions. "You devil! You devil!" She turned on James and began beating him with her fists.

He put his hands up to protect himself but she went on beating him, over and over again, until he let himself fall backwards on the ground. She jumped to her feet and started kicking him. Then she threw the chair at him as he lay there, huddled. "I hate you, I hate you!" she cried. "You're terrible! You're awful. You're disgusting! You're a traitor. You're a worm. You're just —" She fell onto him and started to beat him again. "I hate you, I hate you, I hate you!" she cried over and over again.

At last James grabbed her arms and held them. "Go on, Catherine, everything you say I deserve. But just —"

She struggled to elude his grasp.

Tears welled into his eyes. "Just... try to find somewhere in your heart to forgive me."

Catherine, held in his tight grip, finally relaxed and let her body fall onto his. Her moans came loud, heart-rending, surrounding James with such feelings of despair. But he did not for a moment release his grip.

As she quietened, he kept his arm around her.

With her free arm she made a half-hearted attempt to strike him again, but gave up.

"I'm so glad it's out," he said. "It's all over now..."

"Not quite."

Oh-oh. So that was it. Would she be taking off for New Carlisle? Leaving him? Couldn't he have kept quiet a while longer? At least, until they knew each other better. Until she trusted him more. No, he had been forced into it, really. "Why not?"

"I have something I've been meaning to say."

His blood curdled. Yes, this confession must have been the last straw. She was going to say she had to end it all. He knew it. His dreams folded into blackness. No more being a married settler, no more hope. "I know, I know Catherine, it's too hard here."

"No, not too hard. But —"

"And I know I should never have asked you. I don't deserve you. I don't deserve anything." Odd, after all they had been through, to have it all end so quickly. "You're going home."

"No, but..."

"But what?"

"James," she rolled over and looked at him. "You've seen I've not been well the past few days. I didn't want to tell you. I thought it would pass."

James was silent. What was coming?

"I think now, it was the sickness of a baby in the making."

His heart leapt and blood flooded his cheeks. What news!

"I did so want to tell you properly," Catherine said. "I'm sorry it had to be like this."

"Don't for one second be sorry, Catherine, I am absolutely thrilled. Just thrilled." He sat up and took up her hand and kissed it over and over. "It is so very, very exciting."

"Is it, James? Are you really happy?"

"How can you ask that?"

She dropped her eyes. "Should we not have waited, perhaps? Waited until at least one winter went by."

"Of course not, Catherine. The sooner, the better." He leaned back. "We must not procrastinate any longer. New

Carlisle is the only place to have the baby — midwives, your mother, neighbours. Yes, we must go there..."

A beatific smile graced her features. "Thank you, James, thank you. I knew you would understand. New Carlisle for the winter." She paused, smiling again. "I'm feeling better already."

Chapter Eighteen: 1813–14

Heavy cloud cover muffled the scene as James paddled his canoe over the opaque, solid-seeming water toward New Carlisle. The two figures in the canoe appeared in silhouette — Catherine, motionless, in the bow shrouded in her dark cloak, and James behind, in his heavy Micmac coat, thrusting the canoe forward with steady strokes.

"You all right, Catherine?" he asked.

"Very all right, thank you, James." Catherine glanced back at her husband, and then returned to her stillness, lost in thought, as was James.

Between them, the loaded canoe hung deeply in the water. They had decided on leaving this day because the harsh winter was approaching. Snow had begun to fall on and off during the past week, and Catherine had lent James a hand preparing to leave. Several trips to the canoe had James stowing their belongings under part of a canvas sail bartered in New Carlisle. His tools had been carefully stashed in his hidden compartment by the brook.

"I've been thinking all about what you told me," Catherine said. James caused hardly a ripple in the ice-flat surface, so expert had he become in manoeuvring the finely fashioned craft. "I can see how you were close to this woman for the long winter. You only did what was natural. And you weren't aware of how much I longed to see you again. Who could blame you?" She turned to look back at him. "James, you are my husband, and we shall put all this Micmac past behind us. We shall work to make it disappear. I accept being your second wife — but no one else shall know."

James took this in with welling happiness. "It will remain unspoken, my love. Does this mean you might see my Micmac friends in a new light?"

"That may take a deal of time, James..."

At peace once more, James found his mind wandering. His thoughts became entwined with the *Flight into Egypt*: his wife in her shawl, a baby on the way, motionless, fleeing a future of deprivation, and he, a modern Joseph, propelling them toward a safe haven, two lonely silhouettes in the dusk. Did it not resemble that biblical scene told in the stone chapel of Raby Castle? Flight into safety, purposeful, silent, gliding smoothly into a new unknown. Were they not, here in the New World, poised on that very same edge between life and death? Yes, he must continue his practice of regular prayer and thanksgiving even more rigorously?

Night was falling and he welcomed the early darkness. He lifted his face to the sky to let the lazy flakes fall upon his cheeks and his outstretched tongue, tasting the winter's nectar. Manna from above, from Him who bestowed all good things. James breathed his thanks. And with his mind drifting, he was given another vision as he stroked surely forward.

Monstrous shapes began to materialize in the falling dark, could they be ships? No sails, steel-crafted, odd chugging like the pulleys and belts that shook the mill, as though some yet-to-be invented motor were propelling them. As these ghostly emanations passed, he fancied he saw sailors high on the decks, waving down at their canoe.

And more yet, as another twilit image began to form: his own house, fully built, solid, with a wide veranda along the front, and who is that emerging — an old man, with a walrus moustache. And there, a white-haired lady, rocking and knitting. Catherine? Yes, perhaps, in her later years. He was coming to sit beside her on a straight-backed chair, looking out over his garden. Would that might come to pass, he thought! How nourishing.

Catherine broke into his reverie. "James do you know where we're going?"

"Of course, my love. Can't you hear waves lapping on the shore?" He held his paddle up, poised in mid-stroke as she cocked her head to one side, and shook her head. Perhaps his months with the Micmac gave him height-ened hearing. And even seeing into the future, as he had just glimpsed. The *Buowin* had told him, he remembered now, that everyone had this gift. One only needed to pre-pare, and then, more important, to listen and watch.

"Your family will be shocked at our arrival," he murmured.

"They may well have been expecting us." She gave a light laugh that forbade rejoinder.

Before too long, James made out the lantern on a pole marking the New Carlisle floating jetty. He brought the canoe in and, leaving their supplies for the moment, they made their way up the slope through the lightly falling snow toward the village. When they reached the shelter of Garretts' darkened veranda, Catherine tried the door.

"Locked," she whispered. "But I have a way." She

pulled at a tab of string high up and the bar lifted. "I'd rather not wake them at this late hour. Then we'll never get to sleep."

They tiptoed inside. Catherine lit a whale oil lamp from embers in the open fire, and assembled their bed beside it. Worn out, they arranged their wet garments around the fire and lay down, too tired to make love.

Before James gave himself up to his great fatigue, his worries arose in all their awesome power. How hard it now would be to tell her family about his other son, John. A "half-breed" is what they'd call him. Would they ever accept the child? Of course not. So what should he do? How would he ever resolve it?

***

The next morning over breakfast, news of the impending birth pleased the Garretts, eliminating any misgivings about the couple's foolhardy plans to winter alone in Shegouac. Catherine did prattle on about her new home, which pleased James, though the Garretts seemingly less.

"Well, you came in good time, laddie," William Sr. said as he lifted his bulk from the table. "I just signed a contract for supplying lumber to the new courthouse they're building. I have need of a good few men in the woods. I'm not too keen to send my sons, but perhaps you'd like to join us in this enterprise."

"Good idea, sir," replied James. What else did he have? Though it would mean leaving Catherine in the town while he went off to work, she'd be with her family for her first important pregnancy. Perhaps rather a good idea.

"Why not us, Father?" little Joseph chimed in.

"Dangerous out there, son. Long way from help. No doctors. Not a midwife around. None but the men working next to you."

"Tough," young Will chimed in. James looked up. Was he trying to lord it over his young brother?

"Aye, tough it is, lad. One swipe o' the axe, and you could be done for. Look at that poor Hardie McGuire..."

"What happened to him?" James asked.

"Bled to death he did, one crack o' the axe and that was it."

"You don't mind if James bleeds to death, Father?" Catherine asked pointedly.

"I'm not going to bleed to death, Catherine," James said. "I worked all one winter in the woods back of Paspébiac with Robin's."

"Aye, and how many of you made it through?" William looked at James.

"All but one. An unfortunate accident, really. A big branch. As one of the trees went down, a branch struck the poor man on the head. Done for. But if you're careful..."

"Of course, of course, you'll all have to be careful, and I'll see you get your share of boards, as deserved. Got to look ahead. No thought of building a proper house for my daughter yet?"

"Lots of thoughts," Catherine said. "But we're hard put to see how it could happen without a deal of help."

This was greeted by silence — ominously so, James thought. No one rushing to volunteer. But that could all change.

***

James loved the crunching noise snowshoes made as he and John Garrett strode over the hardened surface of the snow, as they had done each day for the past two months. It reminded him of his winter with the Micmac, ferreting out the best rabbit and other small-game runs to set their snares on their trapline.

No snow had fallen for a couple of weeks in these February woods far back behind New Carlisle, and the sheeted surface, thawing from a bright midday sun and freezing again at night, now gave off a faint sheen in the grey monochrome of dawn. All was silent, naught stirring save three teams, two young men each, leaving the bunkhouse after a breakfast of porridge, bread, and molasses. John and Will Jr. had prevailed upon their father to let them come, for they planned on building a boat before too long and needed lumber for that. Will Garrett had been paired as an older partner. The third pair had been conscripted by Garrett on a trip to Paspébiac: Alphonse and Abelard.

They had all come back on a horse-drawn sleigh to the camp some fifteen miles behind Hall's mill, on what was becoming known as Hall's River. James had brought his firearm and William had his father's, which dated back to Revolutionary days when he fought for the British. These firearms allowed them to shoot small game, so that they need only send a horse and sleigh every couple of weeks from New Carlisle for supplies.

James and John walked along a horse-road that led out from the central bunkhouse like spokes of a wheel. They reached their own neatly stacked logs waiting to be skidded by horse to the riverbank and floated down in the spring flooding. The log booms would then arrive at

Hall's mill to be sawn into planks for the new court-house.

Today, the Gaspé cold had come bearing down: breath formed clouds of vapour that condensed on eyelids and eyebrows and stung their faces. James could almost hear the frosty air pinging around them — so snapping cold! The limbs of trees cracked as they moved. Hard chopping today, James thought, those logs'll be frozen like rocks. Be on guard! Remember the accidents in the woods back of Paspébiac! When it was this cold, axes glanced off wood as if it were granite.

"John," he said, turning, "we'll have to be careful, it's biting cold out."

"Just thinking the same thing."

James and John cut trees just far enough from the road so that the eight-foot logs could be upended and easily piled in cords on each side of the track. Once they'd chosen their strip, they took a number; each team put their own mark on their pile with keel, a black marker somewhat like chalk. The scaler would come every month and tot it up. That way, James was both working for Garrett and for himself, so that he'd have logs for the spring when he intended to begin on the house. He had some lumber accumulated from the summer's work at the mill, as well.

James walked ahead of John, expert on snowshoes after his winter back on the plateau of the caribou. How he loved this part of the day when the soft gauze of dawn light filtered out harsh edges; black trees stood like exclamation marks on white sheets of snow, such stately guardians, stiff, formal, bearing messages from passing millennia as they awaited their unwritten fate. Could

James divine what it was? The Micmac might know.

Imagine, James would be making his house from these messengers. What a joy to have these carriers of age-old messages folded around in walls and above him in planks for the ceilings, and above that, in a peaked and shingled roof. Could the old stones of Raby Castle boast the same legacy? Perhaps. Having lain in their rocky ridges for millennia, they might carry messages, too. But he doubted it. Nothing like wood, he told himself as he crunched his way along the broken trail, axe in one hand, saw in the other, anticipating a good day's work. A happy man, taking his first steps toward the building of their future home in Shegouac.

Chapter Nineteen: Spring 1814

Hammering rung out across the building site above Shegouac brook. John Gilchrist, New Carlisle's finest cabinet-maker and carpenter, had agreed to help them, together with his son. And prodded by his father and mother, Will Jr. had agreed to come to Shegouac with a close friend while John managed to enjoin two others. Young Joseph, now sixteen, had needed no encouragement, and finally Ben had begged Mr. Hall to give him leave for a fortnight to join the fun. Mr. Garrett himself collected on an old debt to persuade a coastal skipper to bring the lumber.

"I'm so happy to have Ben with me," Catherine confessed, after the first day's feeding of the men. "We'd be hard put to harvest enough vegetables, even in these early spring woods, to add to the salt fish Mother gave us. Washing and tidying after meals, too, it's a big job."

"Big job indeed," agreed James, eyeing his wife's protruding belly. "I'm afraid it might be too much for you. Perhaps you should have stayed behind."

"And if I had, how on earth would you have managed?"

James shrugged. "No idea. But I'm worried about your condition."

"Don't be. We pioneer women are tough!" She gave a cheerful grin and went on with her work.

One of the first things they did was dig a pit for the

rip-saw with its eight-foot-long blade. One man worked down in the pit and another on top, each pulling the wooden handles in turn. Posts held the log steady while the two men sawed down the length, splitting off rough planks.

One lunchtime James saw Will and his close friend sitting conspicuously apart, engaged in low conversation. He did not like the look and nudged Catherine.

Putting down his plate, he drew himself up and strode across the building site with Catherine. "Is there a problem?"

William flinched slightly as Catherine turned, eyes flashing. "I think my brother is jealous!"

"I am not!"

"Then why are you so against this building?"

William shrugged. "Well, I do wonder, dear sister, why my father, who fought so nobly for the British, has only a small piece of land, fifty acres, and James here —"

"— has a good deal more?" James intervened. "William," he began gently, but not without a hint of steel, "all the waste land from Paspébiac to Pabos is yours for the taking."

"It may be here for the taking now, but when that land commission they talk about starts investigating, you might find it's damn well *not* for the taking."

"That may be." James struggled to keep his composure. "But now it is, and you are welcome to come and settle anywhere. What about that piece on the other side of the brook? It's good land. I've surveyed it. It would be fine for some young family —"

"Do you think I'd be crazy enough to live this far away? What if my wife had a child, as Catherine is doing? How would she manage here all alone? What if something went wrong — say I broke an ankle and couldn't walk. What if you slashed yourself with your axe, like poor Hardie McGuire? You'd be done for. No sir. Definitely not for me."

John joined in. "You know, William and I are thinking of building a ship together. Lots of money in carrying freight along this coast, James."

James nodded. But these warnings that Will was voicing — he had a point. This was indeed a perilous existence, far from any neighbours. Others might come soon, but how soon? More likely, the Gaspé settlements would actually get smaller, the deprivations being well known abroad. Not many were willing to lead such a harsh life.

Those settlements below the border were a whole other kettle of fish. The weather there was less extreme, the population had doctors and officers of the law to help them, and men schooled in the sicknesses of animals; Old Country crafts were also flourishing. Up here, this "savage, uncivilized and barbaric" coastline was without such means of support.

"You don't have to live here, William," Catherine added. "There is plenty of land available near New Carlisle. When the time comes for you to build your house and barn, James will be delighted to help. You know that very well."

Other workers nearby nodded their accord. Here in the New World, everyone helped each other.

"But look at the size of what we're trying to build," Will argued. James had planned two buildings: the house, with a downstairs room to serve as kitchen and general living area, and a large upstairs bedroom to be divided later; and a barn for which James had been squaring timbers; he had become handy with a broad axe. "What are you going to do with it all?" Will went on. "You've got no arable land I can see. How long do you think it will take to get a farm going? Years and years. You've bitten off more than you can chew, that's what I say. I hate working with no end in sight."

"Now you listen to me, Will," Catherine said, eyes flashing. "We'll get an ox next year, and watch how quick our land will get cleared then. We'll have children, and they'll help. Why build half a house? We need a whole one right now. If you're so against it, just go back to Father."

James could see Will had no desire to face an irate North Country father. But he wondered if he had, in fact, not bitten off too much. He straightened. "So why don't we stop for a few minutes?" They had been working since sunrise. "Let's do as the Navy does: break out the rum."

After producing a keg, he and Catherine went from person to person, dolling a splash into their wooden piggins. On his ship's deck, the ten-gallon tub of rum had letters: "The King — God bless him" carved into it for their edification, though not many crewmen could read.

The keg went round, finishing with the piggin of little Ben. With his one good hand, he raised it to his lips and drank to the last drop.

***

"Now where's all them trunnels?" Gilchrist asked, as he stood surveying the work, eyeing the site with his carpenter's practised eye.

James screwed up his face. "Trunnels?"

"'Tree nails,' you sailors'd call 'em, you got none made?"

"I don't think..."

"Murray, better get to work, laddie! Show James."

"Sure will, Poppa." His son grinned at James.

"You take a piece of this here wood, left over, and you split it with your froe, here." He handed James the L-shaped chisel, blade at right angles to the handle, "to get small pieces. Now you shape them." He winked at John, who already knew this. "On this here shaving horse," which he had carried up from the rowboat, "you use a drawknife. Now see the cross-piece on the pivot, below the bench? When you step on it," he demonstrated by pushing his feet forward, "the head comes down and pins the piece of wood you're making into your trunnel, so's you turns it. So now, you shave it," demonstrating, "and turns it," he worked at it deftly, easily, "till you get a little taper on it, and here! Yer perfect trunnel."

James fingered the wooden peg. So the mystery of the nails was solved. You used wooden trunnels. All sizes and shapes.

Within a week, Gilchrist had the completed four walls of the house laid out on the ground. "All hands to the pump!" They gathered around, Ben too. "Right, south wall up first!" One after another, with some heaving and lots of loud exhortations, the four walls were raised.

James stood back, inordinately proud of his house on its rock foundations. His whole adventure had come to a head. Catherine took his hand as they stood in admiration.

"Mr. Gilchrist, you achieved the impossible. Catherine and I thank you from the bottom of our hearts."

"Och, 'twas nothing. Glad to be of help. Right now, lads, barn rafters next!"

***

How on earth can you stabilize roof rafters without any iron spikes or nails? James wondered out loud.

"Mortise and tenon." Gilchrist hefted a beam with a square hole at one end. "Your mortise is a rectangular socket, like this here."

"And the tenon?"

"The tenon is that there finger." He picked up another rafter with a smaller square end shaped into it. "This squared end goes into the socket, the mortise."

"Looks okay, but how do you —"

"Well, yae drive in the tenon with this here beetle." He picked up a huge mallet. "You swing it between your legs." Gilchrist straddled the beam and swung the mallet: tuck tuck tuck, it sounded. "You knock this here beam, well, the tenon, into the mortise of the big beam."

"Easy when you do it."

"Now here's the best bit. You drill a hole through them both, see?" He leaned hard on the drill's rounded handle, and with a mighty arm circled it so that it drilled a hole through the centre of the fitting. "Your trunnel goes through this here hole in the middle, and holds them together good."

With that mystery solved, James thought his house would be amongst the most solid on the Coast. Mr. Gilchrist surely knew his trade. But James's delight was cut short when another argument split the peaceful workers. James put down his heavy axe and walked over.

"No siree," John was saying, "my sister's not climbing that ladder every night with a tiny baby!"

"But John, 'tis a fine ladder," Will countered, "easy to climb. That's how all houses start. You never put in a staircase at first." Hot under the collar, Will began to shout. "Ask Gilchrist."

James hesitated. It was his decision, but the two brothers were his prime helpers. He held out his hands. "Just explain, John. Where would we put a staircase?"

As Will frowned, John pointed to the northeast corner. "Nothing easier. We set it in that corner. Four steps up toward that north wall, then turn and go up along the west wall. Underneath that, we make a closet. Handy to store things. I could put shelves..."

"Sure, we could put shelves everywhere and cupboards and make this a palace. We just don't have time!" Will shouted.

James felt John was in the right, but so was Will. "How would it be then, if you began the steps and I finished them off later?"

"Good, James," John said, taking over. "That fine ladder will be great in the barn, Will, where no one climbs with babies into the loft after eggs."

The argument was interrupted by Catherine, who called out, "Dinner!" She dolloped out stew in the bowls.

"What's in this?" Will asked.

"Never you mind. I'll tell you later."

James knew she had made the stew with cattail roots from the Hollow. Not everyday fare for New Carlislers, but certainly a delicacy for the Micmac. They all tucked in but James could not ignore the fact that Catherine seemed more out of breath after climbing the hill. The due date of the baby approached.

***

That trauma of his first wife's death in childbirth kept haunting James. He knew his fears to be mainly groundless, so back in New Carlisle, James was only too happy to settle in with the brothers, helping the Garretts do their spring planting — anything to get his mind off his panic at the looming birth.

One evening, exhausted from the long days, he came back with the brothers. As they washed up at the table out along the back wall, the look on his mother-in-law's face told him everything. "On its way?"

"Seems like it," Mrs. Garrett responded. "Catherine is upstairs with the midwife. I have a fire going for hot water. All is well. You and the brothers will eat tonight next door at the neighbours'."

"May I see her?" asked James

"Of course, but don't stay long. This is women's business."

James went in and climbed the stairs in mounting terror, but he cheered up when he saw Catherine in her new nightgown, comfortable in her parents' bed. All the lamps in the house had been assembled and stood unlit upon the chest of drawers. He came forward anxiously. "How are you doing, my love?"

"Quite well, thank you, James. But please, try to appear happy."

"We all are," the midwife chimed in. "Merciful Lord, it's a blessed occasion, indeed it is."

James hadn't realized how clearly his concern showed.

All the same, her reprimanding tone of voice struck him like a blow.

"No no, of course. Forgive me." He tried to smile. "This will be the happiest night of my life," he lied. For he was swamped by a sickening gloom, might he never, ever see her again? He watched, helpless, as his beloved wife twisted in the fierce pain of a contraction.

Almost as quickly as it came on, it disappeared. The midwife said cheerfully, "That's soon, dearie. 'Twill not be long. So off you go, Mr. Alford."

He and Catherine locked eyes in a loving connection. Then he turned, and stepped heavily downstairs.

The brothers were waiting for him. They got up in anticipation. "We got a surprise for you, James." John gathered round with the others. "Gonna be fun."

"Yes, lots of fun," Will chimed in. "We all want to celebrate with yez. Not every day a fellow's sister gives birth to a baby! So let's get going!"

"Oh well, I think perhaps I'll just —"

"You'll just nothing!" laughed John and grabbed James by the arm. "Come on now, we've got your house built for you, you're coming to celebrate."

So off the four young men went, down the muddy main street and north up a side road. Will led them to a shack half buried in the woods, where men sat on rough benches, quaffing pints of rum and homemade beer. As they were settling themselves, a rough-looking oaf came out and Will called, "Innkeeper! Your finest rum. My sister's having a baby. We're here to celebrate!"

Innkeeper? Hardly a denomination James would have used — the fellow appeared more like a pirate or a rum-runner. James looked around. No moon, but lots of stars flashing bright across the blackness. On rough tables sat whale-oil lanterns.

The rum appeared, and they each helped themselves to a good slug. James sipped at his, just to show he was one of the boys. "Now what are these plans you have for building a ship, John?"

"Maybe in a year or two we're gonna get Mr. Day to help us build a coastal schooner."

"And Will, you'll be master?"

"No siree, that's John. Me, I'm only a farmer. Oh, I'll sail along the first year, just to see my little brother gets to no harm!" He nudged him in jest. And the two set about arm wrestling, after throwing down a challenge. Oddly enough, John won.

After a while, James rose. "Well, I'm off. This was a real celebration! Thanks so much." All three rose to protest. "No, I've really got to get back. Rum doesn't sit well tonight." He gave a rueful smile.

After another round of protests James took his leave, and headed back.

***

The sky above James glittered with a million stars. He sat, legs outstretched on the bare planks of the floating dock and leaned back against a stanchion. The high-masted schooners rocking at anchor had a calming effect. High above to the south, he saw Orion striding across the sky with his trusty dog, Canis Major. Sirius, the Dog Star, seemed especially bright. Even Canis Minor was trotting calmly along behind, clearly visible.

He tilted his head back further to see the fixed pole

star. The rectangle of Ursa Major, the Great Bear, seemed to be ambling happily across his darkened woods, paying little attention to his companions. Hydra, twirled snakelike around the North Star, served to remind James of the evil and misfortunes that sometimes befell, not only sailors, but landlubbers. He shut his eyes quickly.

A time for prayer. If the baby were born healthy, he would write his mother again. He had spoken with Catherine and the next year they would bring her over for sure. Catherine said she would welcome the companionship, especially a hand with chores and the baby. William Sr. had said that he might help with the passage, for he too was pleased that another grandparent might accept to come to that god-forsaken spot. He presumed she was of good stock, though James had been careful to speak of his British background only in the vaguest terms.

James checked upwards again, and saw the gentle Cassiopeia in her rocking chair, knitting calmly. Had she been there knitting for all time? So far as he knew, she would do so far into the future. Perhaps the image calmed him, for suddenly he sat up with a shock. How long had he slept? Orion had been replaced by the noble Boötes. How awful! To drift off while his wife was in labour. With a wave at the great inventor of ploughs and his lovely bright star, Arcturus, James hurried over the broad meadow, peopled as always with the sleeping forms of cattle and sheep. Then he slowed down, heart sinking. All was dark and silent. Like a tomb? Even the dead seemed to be moving in wisps about the town. The long-dead shades of the first settlers: had Catherine already joined their ghostly throng? He turned along the Garretts' street. On the corner he saw the house, but all the windows were lit. Were they even now laying out her body? He almost cursed himself for his lack of faith. Ah well, the moment had come: he must, like Caesar, cross his Rubicon. He mounted the steps.

Sounds of jollity, whoops of joy. Could this be true? He strode quickly to the door and threw it open. Everyone was in there, neighbours included, celebrating.

"The happy father! Come in, come in. Run upstairs. Catherine has been asking for you. She's really worried. Where have you been? Run up quick."

He needed no second urging. Up he went, and there she lay, the baby in her arms. "Well, James, we did it! It's a girl."

Chapter Twenty

Soon after the baby girl's birth, James decided to return alone to finish the half-completed house. Catherine should remain a while longer before bringing her newborn into the wilderness. They had named her Mariah: Mary, the mother of his Lord. An acknowledgement.

Once back in Shegouac, he knew he must first visit his other baby, John, in the Micmac community behind Port Daniel. He found the band in fine spirits and decided to stay two days this time, especially wanting more time with his son, and with the aging Tongue, whom he found slowing down somewhat. Sunrise had gone back with her husband to the encampment at the mouth of the bay in Listiguj.

He bartered items for a new bow and arrow; this winter with Catherine and Mariah he'd need meat for sure. With his musket he might bag a moose, but remembering his nearly fatal encounter back in the Highlands, James determined to hedge his bets and get a spear. He did reveal details of his new wife, though not of their daughter. Soon he'd start the difficult, perhaps even impossible, negotiations to fetch his Native son for integration into a white settler's life.

Two weeks later, at work on his own barn roof, James saw a boat rowed by two sturdy men and poised between them, a woman holding a baby. Catherine! He scrambled down the ladder and raced to the brook's mouth. Any doubts were cast aside — Mariah must be healthy for Catherine to come home this early.

And what an arrival! Wading out into the waves, he picked her up and carried her and Mariah ashore as her brothers John and Joseph pulled the rowboat up onto the beach.

"I'm sorry, James, I just couldn't wait. I didn't want you to miss one minute of your daughter's growth. Look, even in three weeks, hasn't she grown?"

Indeed she had. "Thank you Catherine, thank you so much." Delighted, he led them back along the trail, the brothers carrying additional food supplies.

William Sr. had finally promised his son the where-withal to begin his boat. So now, with the spring planting over, John was spending a couple of weeks here helping James on the house. He wanted to learn something from James of the lore of the sea, and any seafaring yarns. And so John and James worked together, first making the farmhouse a fitting establishment for the lady Catherine and her lovely daughter. Young Joseph had rowed the boat back the next day.

While they worked around, James let his newly bought chickens loose to scratch among the trunks for sustenance. So easy to feed and keep. Eggs for the summer; Catherine's idea was bearing fruit. He especially loved the sound of the rooster waking him in the mornings as he slept on the rough boards by the fire. He'd gotten a rooster so the eggs would produce more chicks. During the winter, Catherine could butcher a hen every couple of weeks to augment their supply of meat. Already it was beginning to feel like a farm.

"You know, James," asked John, "with this here barn getting ready, when are ya going to get yourself some animals?"

"An ox, an ox is first. But how can I ever pay for it?"

"Scarce as hens' teeth, them baby oxen," John agreed. "I'll watch out for one, but every calf — well, the owners want them for themselves. Impossible t'buy, I'd say. Them that can afford one, they's after one, too."

"So I've seen."

"Any bull calves to spare, the farmers butcher in the autumn. Gotta get food somehow."

James nodded. "But without an ox, how can I clear my land?"

"Now James, where's the tar?" John changed the subject. "With the barn roof finished —"

"Tar? I'd forgotten. Oh dear!"

"A roof without tar, how long do you think it'll last in our weather?"

James knew tar from his sailing days and working on Robin's barque. This meant an urgent trip to Paspébiac.

So when the day came for John to leave, James paddled him up to New Carlisle and stopped at Paspébiac on the way back.

"I've come to buy a barrel of pitch," James said, as he walked up to the counter of the Trading Post he'd first visited with the Micmac.

The trader remembered him from the time James had borrowed a leather hat as a disguise, when on the run from the British Marines, and had returned it promptly. "Got any tar?" James asked. "Pitch for roofs?"

The trader nodded. "Take time. Maybe tomorrow."

Yes, thought James, you'll fetch it at Robin's and then

sell it to me for double the price. Pity I can't go myself —
they only work in the truck system, he knew. "How
much?"

"Half a barrel, one *livre*."

A pound sterling, James told himself, double the ten
shillings he had planned on. He sighed. "All right, thank
you."

He paused to join with the men who stood around the
stove in sombre conversation.

"You not hear the news?" one said. "A man, he found
dead on beach. Jump off cliff."

"Someone dead? Who?"

"Young fella. *Il voulait être fermier*. He want become
farmer, him. Live back in woods. He start to clear land.
Now all finish, for sure."

So this had been the topic of their bleak discussion.
And indeed, for Paspébiac, big news. Curious that someone would have jumped over the cliffs. Not at all like a
settler. *"Est-ce qu'il s'est suicidé?"*

"Peut-être. Me, I t'ink bad things happen. *Tout le
monde pense la même chose,"* answered the man.

Bad things indeed, James reflected, and they all
agreed. Then, his eye was caught by a curious sight.
Huddled in the corner, lifeless, but twitching an ear: a
calf? Three or four weeks old, he guessed. "What's that?"

"She for sale. But no one buy, I think. Half-dead."

James went over to the little calf and knelt. The calf
tried to lift its weak head to look at him. He reached out
and scratched it behind the ear. What a shame. He
looked closer. A bull calf.

Just what he needed! His mind whirled. Dying, obviously, so it couldn't cost much. How did it get here?

He rose and went to the counter. "Who is selling it?"

"*Tu veut l'acheter?*"

"I might buy it, depending on price." Should get it for a shilling or two, he thought. But he'd like to know a good deal more. Had it been stolen?

"For sure. De owner, he come soon," the trader told James.

James went back to the little calf. Thin, but nice red and white markings. Not well looked after. Who knows, he thought, could it be rescued? An ox for his farm — how long had he dreamed of that? But his money — he needed that for pitch.

Through the open door walked the scrawniest, mean-est individual James had seen in a long time. Long scraggy hair, a slight but wiry frame, black beard, and clothing that had not been washed for ages. James looked down into his darting weaselly eyes.

"*Tu veut achêter mon boeuf?*" the man asked.

"*Peut-être.*" James went on in French: how much do you want?

"*Cinque livres,*" the man replied.

"Five pounds? Go on! You must be joking."

"No joke," said the man. "Fine bull calf. Make ox one day for farmer."

"Half-dead," James replied in French, thinking fast. All he had in the world he had brought with him, thirty shillings. "I'll give you ten shillings. Gonna die any minute."

The weasel stared him up and down. "Never she die. Thirty."

James waited, thinking, and then nodded. "All right, I'll give you twenty but that's all."

"You got de money now?" asked the weasel. "You give me now, I give you calf. Then you go. Where you bring?"

"Oh, I have a canoe down at the wharf," James replied without thinking. "I'll carry him down." Then he thought, why did he ask that? And why did he agree so quickly on the price? Something did not add up.

The weasel held out his hand.

The men around had stopped talking and were watching; the innkeeper leaned forward on his counter.

"All right," James responded. "I'll be back in a minute." And out he went.

He was not going to let the weasel see where he kept his money, which Catherine had sewn into his waistband. He leaned against the log wall and with the knife he still carried Micmac fashion round his neck, he slit a stitch and pulled the thread. The waistband opened and he took out the money. Was he being foolish? Spending their hard-earned money on a bull calf that might die at any minute. But something told James it might just be the chance he'd been counting on. Then and there, he grew determined to save the little bull's life. Resolutely, he walked back into the store.

"Here." He handed over the precious twenty shillings.

The weasel's eyes glowed. He grabbed the money, thrust it in his pocket, and ran out quickly. In the doorway he paused. "You go now your canoe?" he asked.

"Later this afternoon. I have some business first."

Why did he let him know that, he asked himself. Well, he was not used to such shenanigans. The first thing, he decided, was to visit Monsieur Blanquart and beg some gruel for the calf before the long journey back to Shegouac. Afterwards, he would return for his roof pitch.

James walked over and picked the calf up, finding it heavier than he expected. Sixty pounds anyway. He hiked it up into his arms and out he went, down the wooded lane toward the shack of M. Blanquart. When he reached the door, he set the little fellow down, trying to make it stand, but it crumpled. "You like it closer to the earth, huh?" Starving, thought James, and knocked on the door.

No answer. He paused, and then in the custom of the time, opened the door. The room was much as he had seen it the year before: tiny models of ships on the worktable, a bunk, and over the open fire, a kettle, still steaming. So M. Blanquart could not be far away. James went through his meagre shelves and found some oats, roughly hand-milled for porridge. That would do. He put some in a bowl with hot water from the kettle, and brought it to the calf.

The little bull smelled it, but did nothing. "Come on, little calf, eat. It's good for you."

But eat it would not. Probably never drunk out of a bowl, James thought. Probably so far just suckled its mother, who now would be either dead or faraway. What could he do? He placed the bowl again under its nose. Nothing happened.

Monsieur Blanquart arrived at the edge of the clearing and stopped short, seeing a stranger. James turned his head and saw the old man run off. He rose quickly. "Monsieur Blanquart! *C'est moi!*"

M. Blanquart hurried forward and embraced him. "*J'avais peur,*" he told James, and went on to explain that there had been strange goings-on recently. A man had been found dead on the beach, and he, like many others, suspected foul play.

James explained about the calf, and M. Blanquart knelt. With practised fingers, his friend daubed gruel on the bull calf's nose. The calf licked it off. Then he put his hand in the bowl and stuck two fingers up to resemble teats.

The calf inspected them, smelled them, and then dipped his little chin into it and began to suckle. James grinned broadly. "M. Blanquart, you have the touch!"

The old man nodded, and James sat back. Now maybe it would live. The calf had a broad red slash across its face, a pink nose surrounded by white. One ear was red, the other white. His ribs showed through. How long had he been like this? And where had he come from? Had there been dirty work at the crossroads? Why hadn't he thrown more questions at the weasel? Well, he would have learned nothing. Perhaps it had been sick and left to die? More likely, it had belonged to the young farmer found dead on the beach.

James handed the now-empty bowl to M. Blanquart, who filled it again and brought it back. This time James himself tried putting his hand in the bowl with two fingers stuck up. The little calf seemed decidedly more perky as it dipped its nose in to suckle. "What am I going to call you?" he asked the little creature.

After two bowlfuls, James saw its eyes fluttering shut, and let it rest. Its head flopped on the ground, and it gave a low moan. "Hope it's not dying..."

"Presque," M. Blanquart said, 'almost,' as he invited James into the shack for a cup of tea. The first subject, before he could speak about the daughter, was the death of the young man found on the beach. M. Blanquart agreed there might have been foul play. Possibly the

young man had been pitched over the bank to make it look like an accident — to avoid the Sheriff and Justice of Peace from New Carlisle coming to investigate. With such evil abroad, James knew he'd better be doubly on guard.

Chapter Twenty-One

James hoisted the bull calf onto his shoulders, draped its four legs round his neck, said good-bye to Monsieur Blanquart, and set off back to his canoe.

He had every reason to be pleased. First of all, the news of Sorrel had been excellent. Apparently one of the Robin's foreign visitors, of good breeding and fine manners, had taken a shine to her. They were now seeing each other in a modest sort of way. She had hoped to see James again, M. Blanquart admitted, but such were the ways here in the New World: people came and went, never sure they'd ever meet again.

Next he'd have to investigate the tar. He decided to put the calf in the canoe and tie its legs to prevent escape, and then go to ask M. Huard. But he'd have to be fast. Dusk was approaching, so no problem paddling back at night, for he knew the coastline.

Carrying the calf, he reached the brow of the hill and started down. A movement on the jetty caught his eye. A man stood up. Could that be the weasel? Another man was with him. They began to move off the jetty toward him. Danger?

He walked swiftly back over the brow, hurrying in spite of his burden. He glanced back to see them break into a run. Where now? No question of going back to M. Blanquart: the old man would be little help against two villains. Hide in the woods? He headed for buildings that backed onto the forest, moving quickly. They were after him, no doubt.

What about hiding in one of the houses he was passing? No time. The occupants might be away, and if he waited for them to answer his knock, the two would be upon him. No, best keep going.

He hurried along the trail between the houses next to the woods, hoping to keep out of sight. It joined a lovers' detour along the cliff. Take that? No. Too easy to catch him, and over the bank he'd go. Probably what happened to the young farmer. Aha! A connection between the weaselly-looking man and the dead body! Had that young farmer bought this same calf? Was the calf a decoy?

James turned and plunged into the woods, going deeper, heading north. With the bull calf on his shoulders, he found it slow going. Fortunately, the overcast sky meant an early darkness. Harder to find him. And then, the calf let out a moan.

James hadn't counted on that. What if it kept on moaning as he ran? They'd hear it for sure. Should he put down the calf and run on ahead? At least his arms would be free, and he could use his knife. But then, if the calf moaned after he left it, they'd take it back. He'd lose both his money and calf.

But escape with his life.

He paused, the calf on his shoulders. He faintly heard running footsteps. He crouched down. Would the calf moan again? He held his breath. Two forms hurried past.

The calf had been silent. But might they not double back soon? He heaved his burden up and set off again, having learned how to move silently through woods, even in fading light. But the calf kept getting heavier.

Don't risk a fight with two rogues more adept than you are at dirty fighting. Keep out of harm's way. But his heart beat strongly, and not just from the running. This was one of those rare times he admitted that, yes, he was afraid.

He crossed the main path to the store, and decided he'd make better time on that. But a short distance ahead, this track met the far end of the cliffside Lovers' Lane. His pursuers would double back, straight at him. He dove off into a screen of thick bushes. Just in time. Before going twenty feet, he heard them come running past again.

As they were passing, he heard: *"Ce maudit anglais,"* they were saying, *"je vais le tuer."* Kill? Kill me? *"Oui oui,"* the other replied, as they ran out of earshot.

He turned east toward Shegouac and hurried along parallel to the road. But the calf let out another pronounced moan. Gotta rest, James thought, and crouched to let the calf off his shoulders. Breathing heavily, he rested beside the animal to regain his strength. Like as not, they'd return with a tracking dog. Just his luck.

James hated fights. That young settler had probably put up a good fight, too. How would James disable them? No, forget fighting, just focus on keeping out of their way.

He got up, scarcely rested, heaved the calf onto his shoulders, and forced himself on through the undergrowth. This wood, being handy to Paspébiac, had been well logged of its old growth, so the thickets and young growth made his going harder. At the same time, it made it harder for them to see him.

He came opposite the trading post.

Should he go in? He edged closer. On the veranda, some men, sounding inebriated, were arguing loudly.

From what he could make out, a second person had been found, badly beaten. Another victim of the same villains?

Head back fast to the canoe? No, they'd have posted a guard, if they had any sense. Or maybe they'd already stolen it. What should he do? Set off toward home? But such a long way. And with this burden? Almost impossible.

After a time, someone came behind him, thrashing the bushes. Without a thought he turned and plunged on. Should he strike for the main road east? He'd make better time. Or just duck down and hide here? What if the calf kept moaning?

As if in answer, the calf did moan, this time louder. James stopped. He heard the thrashing stop. The man had obviously heard, too. Then the movement continued. No question of trying to hide. Just go, go fast. But his knees were giving out.

James looked around, and found a stout dead branch, perfect as a club. He grabbed it and pressed back into the branches of a heavy spruce, leaving the calf in full sight as a trap.

The lumbering brute burst into view. He stopped when he saw the calf. As he bent over it, James whacked him hard. He dropped, senseless. James grabbed up the calf and, still with the club, tore for the road.

His burden grew heavier. He slowed down. In the distance, thunder rumbled. Oh no, not rain! How would his calf survive the long trek to Shegouac in this weather?

He should have left well enough alone. So leave the calf here and save your own life? He dismissed that thought as quickly as it arose — this new prize would bring the farm enormous benefits, were it to live. And he had already developed feelings for the little creature.

And just then, down his neck and across his back, warm liquid began spreading. Oh heavens, it was pissing!

As the wet urine began to chill, he also realized that his pursuers, being faster and having seen their companion clubbed, would double their pace and be on him in no time. He'd better get his strategy straight. The little bull was letting out sporadic moans of discomfort, not enjoying its position draped around James's neck. Enough to alert anyone within range.

C'mon, he told himself, think fast. In his pouch, he carried extra twine for the canoe. Make a tripline? Like the cord the Micmac stretched across their path to warn them of intruders. Why not?

He spotted two trees, not too far apart on either side of the trail. He turned into the woods, put down the calf in the roadway as a decoy, grabbed one end of the twine, and tightened it around one tree trunk. Then he went quickly to the other and started to tie the twine, just as his pursuers ran down the path.

He stretched the cord tight.

The first attacker, the heavy man, went sprawling. The other, the weasel, ran past. James stepped forward and landed a solid blow on the head of the fallen thug.

The weasel stopped and turned. He pulled out a hunting knife, and came at James. Knife versus club. But James felt in no condition to fight, having carried his burden for what seemed hours.

"Hey, *je n'ai plus d'argent sur moi,*" he called out. *"C'est ridicule!"* No money on me! Ridiculous. In French: "I'll let you go. I'll tell no one. You can go back safely."

The weasel lunged. James dodged to one side, and swung his club. The weasel feinted again. He was far more agile than James.

They feinted back and forth, lunging, counterlunging. Panting hard, James lowered his club like a battering ram and ran at his opponent. Confused, the man lifted his knife to strike. James thrust the club's butt end into his gut, but the knife struck James on his shoulder as the man crumpled. James lifted his club again and struck him hard. Not enough to smash the skull. But quite enough to keep him down. Damn, James thought, as blood began running down his chest. Now what?

He threw down the club and went to the nearest pine. A branch had been hacked off when this path had been cleared. With his knife he pried loose some gum, stuck it in his mouth. Then chewing hard, he went back to his opponents who lay motionless. He checked them. Both breathing. The first man began to stir. James picked up his club and whacked him again. He lay senseless.

He took a couple more chews and then pulled the flap of skin tight where the knife had struck. He pressed the gum onto it and held the wound hard, until he felt the trickle slow. He closed his shirt, picked up the calf, draped it round his neck again, and went off. But would the calf live through the night?

***

The rain came down heavier. Good, it would wash away

171

the piss. But also drain what little warmth his calf could muster. Many miles before the Nouvelle River. All night for sure. Death had been stalking them and now should finally catch up. Full of doubts and conflicts, he saw the trail widening. He could even make out in the darkness two distinct ruts, indicating oxcarts. Might there be houses ahead?

He had to stop every so often to put the calf down. Sopping wet, exhausted, he had not eaten; neither had his calf, except for a couple of bowls of porridge. Find a stream, he thought, water would help. And what about his tar left behind? And the canoe? At the jetty. It would be gone by now, he felt sure. Too much to absorb. Just save yourself — and your future worker.

And so on they went, man and burden, for another hour. In the hard rain and low clouds, the night was as black as the tar he hadn't been able to buy. Twice he fell with the calf on his shoulders. The second time he stayed down, resting. What if he sprained an ankle? Or broke an arm? Must be careful. But how, in this utter darkness? Would it be better to huddle under some tree and weather out the night? That way he could impart warmth to the little bull.

No, try to struggle on. The trees were thinning out. More open space. Perhaps some houses? In the east, a pale ledge of light had begun to slide forward under the solid night. Dawn this early? Yes, they were near the summer solstice.

On he struggled. As the light spread upwards and the sky took on a blue-grey cast, he realized this was a made road. How recent? Some open space featured tilled land, and log fences. The Nouvelle River could not be that far away. Hungry, chilled, and worn out, he prayed for some early-rising settler.

He passed a homestead, and peered intently. No sign of life. He kept going. As he neared the river, he saw more tilled land.

With no nourishment since early yesterday, James knew he'd soon have to give up. His legs were giving out. He had to keep putting down his little animal to rest.

Better bang on doors. At the first modest-looking cabin on the bay side of the road, he stopped. He stroked his little bull, wiping off the rain. Still alive, he saw, but only just. He must find nourishment soon. But with the summer solstice at hand, this first light was still middle of the night. Who'd be awake now with a hard day's work ahead? Well, here goes, he thought, and banged on the first door.

Nothing. He banged again, harder, and called out.

A woman inside gave a frightened cry. A man's voice asked in French, "Who is it? Door locked. No come in."

"Please... I'm a settler. I'm bringing home a calf. We need help." He repeated the last phrase in French.

"Go away," the man said, still in French. "We trust no one."

"Please," said James. "I'll back away, you can open the door, see who I am."

"No! Go 'way. *Vas-ten vite*! I have gun. I will shoot."

James sighed, shook his head, and set off again. Shame that even here, lawlessness must reign.

Starving and worn out, James at last saw in the distance a low hill that might hide the Nouvelle River beyond. He picked out a couple of decently constructed houses set well back from the road. Surely one of them would open their door. If not, his little bull was done for.

One good-sized house displayed the faint glow of a whale-oil lamp. He turned in and banged hard. The door opened and a tall, lean settler with a long face, about fifty, stood in the doorway. "Welcome stranger!"

Before replying, James cast his eyes skyward and offered a quick but fervent thanks to His Maker. "I can't believe I've found salvation! You're English?"

The man nodded and came to help him, as James laid down his calf. "Where you from? Them houses other side of Nouvelle?"

"No, much further down. James Alford." He held out his hand.

"John Ross. Come in, come in. Bring that animal in, too. Needs warmth, by the look of it."

What luck! A warm-hearted home with welcoming flames burning in the open fireplace, a cauldron of porridge cooking, and a wife who looked as if she'd cared for many children. The place gave off an air of kindly hospitality. Safe for the moment. If only the bull calf kept living.

Chapter Twenty-Two

James woke up with a start to find Catherine crying out over him, "James, are you all right?"

He tried to collect his thoughts. "Yes yes..." Where was he? Catherine? He must be near home! But what had he been doing? Oh goodness — the calf! He tried to get up, but his legs would not respond.

Catherine bent down, and tried to help him stand. She kept asking, "Whatever happened, James? Where is the canoe? You gave me such a fright, lying there. I had a premonition, you know. Well, first I found these raspberries — a surprise for you. But something just made me come out..." She chattered on as he sat down again, eyes bleary. "I just knew something was wrong. Well, are you all right?" she asked again.

James nodded weakly and, hanging onto Catherine, rose again to look around. "I brought a surprise." Amazing, he had made it after all. After the Rosses, crossing the Nouvelle, soaking, stumbling, losing the little fellow, finding him in the dark waters, tripping again in the sluggish bottom, struggling on, then reaching the bank and walking, walking... He turned and began weakly retracing his steps, Catherine following with the baby on her back. James had improvised a sling for her from old canvas, using the Micmac carrier as an example.

"James, what are you doing?"

"Looking. For a present." Had the calf survived? "Oh dear, where is the little fellow?"

"What little fellow?" Catherine cried in alarm.

"There!" He stopped and pointed.

Catherine gasped. "What is that!"

"Our prize. If it's alive." He knelt. No, the animal had not made it. Lifeless.

James felt its chest. No movement. He knelt close and pressed his ear against its chest. Yes, a heartbeat. He looked up. "Still alive!"

"James," Catherine exclaimed angrily, "what have you done!"

"Brought us a bull calf, Catherine. Just think, our very own bull calf."

Catherine stared. "What do you mean, James, a bull calf? How are we going to feed that? We have just enough to keep us alive. Can't you think of the baby? What on earth have you been doing!" She was furious.

"But Catherine, please, think what it will do! Just what we've wanted all along."

"What good will an ox be to us if we're both dead of starvation?" She turned angrily and threaded her way through the bushes to the raspberry patch, and then headed through the heavy woods ringing their clearing.

James remained kneeling, what little life he had draining out of him. Never for a moment had he dreamed Catherine would be anything but thrilled.

He slumped back and wiped his head. What should he do? Just take the little animal and throw it over the bank? No doubt in his mind Catherine came first. If she didn't want the animal, no matter what he had gone through to get it here, he'd have to get rid of it. But perhaps she just hadn't understood. If she had time to think, perhaps her reaction would change?

At any rate, he stooped and with his last burst of strength he picked up the little animal, lifeless though it seemed, and staggered after Catherine, till he reached the corn and wheat beginning to sprout in the weed-grown earth between low stumps around the house. At the front door, he almost collapsed with the calf.

Catherine appeared, basket of raspberries in hand, eyes flashing. "I suppose you traded our wonderful canoe for that!"

James shook his head. No strength to go into all that now. But one thing he resolved as he stroked the little beast's neck, he would not now let it die. Get rid of it, he might, but right now, he had to find it some food.

"Catherine, I'm sorry. I'm just so hungry." He forced himself up and struggled over to flop at the table by the fire. He glanced up to see her, still in the doorway, looking at him with real concern. Had she begun to see what bad shape he was in?

She hurried to the shelves, got crushed oats and mixed them in a bowl with hot water from the kettle over the fire. She stoked it, adding kindling, and poured the porridge into their spider, a frying pan with legs. "I'm sorry, James, I was so shocked I forgot about my dear husband!"

His head spun as he sat. He'd tell the whole story later. He watched as she moved to the shelves for bread and molasses. "I found your bow and arrow."

"My bow and arrow?" He had hidden them well up by his secret storage compartment. Had she also found the spear? All easily explained — he needed them for hunting this autumn, because only a substantial store of meat would keep them through the winter. A moose. Porcupines. The latter, being such slow movers, he'd pick off with a bow and arrow — not to waste precious shot and powder. But was he strong enough to explain all this just now?

"Well, I learned to shoot with the bow and arrow with the Micmac. I'm not much good. But if I can practice a bit... See, Catherine, so much faster than a firearm. After one gunshot, it takes minutes before you're ready to fire the second. The moose can come and finish you off while you're loading."

"Those were not there before. You went back to the Micmac while I was nursing Mariah."

Well of course he went back. Had he not mentioned it? Oh, perhaps, to avoid that awful truth of his only son. Now, she did suspect something was up. But he was not up to any argument right now. "Yes, of course I did — but Catherine, dearest, can't all that wait till I have something to eat?"

"Oh, James, I'm sorry. But you can see, I'm upset. To think of you running off to your Micmac women while I'm suckling your only child. You can hardly blame me."

So that was it! She was worried about other women. He almost smiled. Easily overcome. But just rambling on about liking Micmac people would do him no good at all. She smelled a rat, as the saying goes. Had the time finally arrived when he would have to tell all? But after her reaction to the bull calf, what would she say about another child? Before he even opened his mouth, he was doomed. He slumped.

Without speaking, she put the porridge down in front

of him, and got him a hot mug. James sipped it. Tea! Saved for special occasions, being so expensive. Well, a spark of optimism. He ate in silence.

"May I have some more bread and molasses?"

"Of course." Catherine rose again, hardly acknowledging the weight of Mariah on her back, asleep. She set the jug of molasses down before James; he poured some onto his plate and scooped at it with another slice of her bread.

Well, everything at once! How could he get her to accept the calf? And then, his son? His mind, weary though it was, groped for answers. He drank his tea and hungrily finished off the bread. "Another slice, please? I'm so worn out, Catherine, I'm sorry. Nothing to eat since yesterday morning."

"I can see that, James, so you just sit, and get your strength back. You'll tell me all about it, when you are able." Good: the old Catherine, whom he loved and trusted, was beginning to reappear. And she asked him about his harrowing experience and he responded. Then he realized, the first thing he must do if this expedition were not to be wasted, was to save the calf. "That little bull calf..." he began. "Can we make some more gruel? Water down the porridge, put in some cornmeal, add molasses, stir it all up. And not too hot." She fell into the wifely mode at once. He finished his tea, and held out his cup. "Another will make me feel better."

Obediently she filled it, and cut another slab of bread, pouring him more molasses.

He looked around. The room was bright with afternoon sunlight. Perhaps all was not lost. Utterly worn out still, he sat and let a shaft of good feelings slide into his heart. The planks of his walls made the room cozy, the ceiling above had been nicely laid from boards ripped out of Hall's mill logs. A lucky man... He might survive. Funny how he had let down all his guard when he reached home. Not at all prepared for her burst of anger. But then, that's the way it was. He had come through such a long night.

Soon, Catherine had readied the gruel.

"We need a wider bowl."

Catherine agreeably found one and stood waiting while he filled it with gruel, and out they went. He knelt at the inert form and lifted the head that lolled in his hands; no strength there, for sure. He daubed gruel onto its nose as Catherine watched. Nothing. He began to whisper gently: a crooning sound. He daubed some more. He waited. Then, surprisingly, a little pink tongue came out and licked. He glanced up at Catherine. She did seem caught up in this life-or-death drama.

He daubed some more. The little tongue appeared again.

"Help," James murmured. "Hold its head above the bowl, like this." He lifted the head and pointed the nose into the gruel.

Catherine knelt, picked up the wobbly head and pointed it down. James stuck his fingers in the gruel and gently pushed the nose onto them. After a time, the calf began to suck. James glanced at Catherine again. Was that a little smile forming?

"Will it live?" she asked.

"We can but hope."

After suckling a bit, the head lolled to one side. "We'll give it a short rest."

Catherine let the calf lie back, and with her fair white hand, began to stroke its cheek.

Later that morning, James carried the little fellow over to its new home in the barn. As he put it down among the stalks and stumps still erupting from the earth floor, Catherine appeared behind. "Shouldn't we get him some straw or leaves to lie on?"

"Yes, definitely, make him comfortable. But first, would you mind bringing the bowl?"

"I have it here." She held it out, but the baby woke up and began to cry.

"I've got to feed Mariah." Catherine left him to deal with the calf.

Deal with the calf, but far more important, deal with his ominous future. When he went back in, he would have to face Catherine with it all: his wife and former family and his son, John.

Chapter Twenty-Three

Late that afternoon, James looked in on his prize, asleep on its fresh cedar boughs, an empty wooden bowl beside. What next? Oh yes, water. James went back to the house and checked the half-barrel's water outside. Nearly empty. He got two buckets and set off down to the brook, feeling a momentary shiver of excitement. Next year, if his bull lived, it would be carrying up the water on its back. He'd have to rig a decent contraption. Talking of rigging, he thought, why not rig myself a simple yoke? A branch, shaped to carry comfortably across my shoulders, with a bucket hanging from each end.

He knelt at the brook, filled his containers, and set off with his burden, but also the bigger burden of how to tell Catherine about his son.

The previous day's journey had taken its toll. His legs felt weak, the buckets of water heavy, whereas he used to carry them easily. But that had given him the idea of a neck yoke, he reflected, so things sent to try us often bring good.

As he gave his calf water, it looked up at him with big brown eyes. Did it know what he had gone through? "You're going to grow into a big strong ox," James said. "You'll help haul water up from the brook. And maybe, by and by, you'll even be pulling a few logs. This winter, I'll feed you fine, don't you worry." Don't worry? He surely did.

And now, what about a name? He found Catherine stirring a stew for their supper, Mariah asleep in her pine cradle.

"Catherine," James began, "what shall we call it?"

"Call what?"

"The calf, of course." Oh-oh, her mind is still on that Micmac trip of his. The new calf hadn't even registered. He was in for it.

"Well, if you're so determined and can figure out how we can manage our long winter ahead, then you can think of a name yourself."

Not making this easy. Nothing would be easy, now. "Maybe we should decide on that when it gets older," he grumbled. "If I don't throw it over the bank first." He was beginning to get angry.

"Why would you throw it over the bank?"

"Because you obviously hate it."

"But I didn't say I hate it. I just asked, how are we going to manage?"

"Once the calf gets its strength, it will be able to stand." His dander was up. "Then, it will graze. Cattle, they eat all sorts of weeds and things. We can give it crushed roots, too, like we eat. Bit of molasses for energy, just for a month or so. I can tether it back to that swale the burn caused last year. Lots of fresh shoots there. No bears this time of year. No wildcats, neither. Anyway, before too long I'll cut feed back there and haul it out on my shoulders. It's a starved little bull now, but when it fattens up, it can last all winter without too much feed. When next spring comes, it'll be out grazing and get back its strength. They're tough animals born here, got to be, to survive."

Catherine looked up. "Sounds reasonable." James could see her relax somewhat. "So, my dearest Catherine, let's please think up a name."

She put the spider on the table and got a few utensils. "Your idea of what it will look like in a couple of years is good. Why not something like Big or Tall or Broad?"

"Broad. That's a good name. I like it." He straightened and pretended he had reins in one hand. "Broad, *gee*," he yelled, which turned an ox right. "Broad, m'son, *haw!*" That turned an ox left. "Sounds good."

Catherine paused by the table, and couldn't prevent a smile. "I can just see you behind him, ploughing our new fields." And then her expression hardened and a lost look came into her eyes. "If we ever see those days..." She turned back to the fireplace, her shoulders sagging. "Food's ready."

Still worried about my Indian concubine, he said to himself. Who doesn't exist. He went out to wash his hands at the outside scrubbing bench. Then, making a decision, he came back and sat across the table. She sat looking at him while James said grace. He took a spoonful of stew.

For a few moments, neither spoke. "Don't you want to know what I've been through?"

She shook her head. "You know what I want to hear, first all." She spooned down some soup, waiting, not meeting his eyes.

"I do, I do, yes," he said. Well, the moment had come. "You remember I told you I had a wife? She only lived with me for one year."

She raised her eyes to meet his. "How could I forget?"

"I thought that was all behind you."

"It was. Until I found the bow and arrow." She dropped her eyes. And returned to her soup.

"I got the bow and arrow, and the spear, when I visited the tribe. We shall need red meat this winter. I shall have to kill a moose, or caribou, to fill our larder. We're not spending another winter in New Carlisle. We've got to make this house work for us. And clearing land is best done in winter. I'll cut like crazy, and next spring, Broad will have logs to skid across the snow."

She looked up. "You're hiding something, James."

True. Well, tell her. Out with it. No more secrets.

"Catherine, I have been... well, afraid to tell you." He took her hands. "I want more than anything to be open with you. I want more than all my heart —"

She pulled away her hands and placed them flat on the table as if to brace herself for the shock.

"Catherine..." He found his voice breaking. How he hated to do this. How much he longed to have her with him forever. And this would shatter that. How could he go on?

She was there, hands pressed hard on the smooth wood. And probably, her heart beating as hard as his.

"Catherine," he began again, "I don't know how to say this."

"James, please, say it anyway. This is killing me." James saw a tear run down her cheek and hit the table. Yes, he had better say it.

"Catherine, I didn't tell you how Little Birch died."

She remained still, listening.

"She died in childbirth." As he said it, the tears started to well up in his own eyes. "I loved her, Catherine. I'm sorry. I did love her. And she died."

Catherine had not moved but her body softened.

He gathered himself. This was so hard. He hated reliving it. He had been so very broken by the whole episode. He repeated, controlling himself. "In childbirth. She had a son."

Catherine lifted her head and looked at him in wonder. They remained silent, while he got a grip on his emotions. "Did he live?"

"Yes." James pressed his hand hard against his mouth. But the tears seeping out told it all. "His name is John. He's a year old. Down there, with his grandmother, Full Moon." He bowed his head and spoke the fateful words: "He is my son, Catherine."

Catherine looked at him across the table, her blue eyes wide with wonder, and also understanding. But James did not see this. For he had placed his forehead on the table and let the sobs come.

She reached out a hand to her husband, who was lost in utter grief.

They stayed like that for a long time, until James could get himself under control. Head still on the table, he mumbled, "And now, there's nothing more to say."

A quick spasm of tears shook him, and he stood up abruptly, and strode out. He crossed his clearing and sat down overlooking the bay, head in hands. Everything was lost, his farm, his wife, his new darling daughter, and his new bull. He wanted to throw himself off the cliff.

Overhead, a few scattered cirro-stratus clouds hung in the falling dusk. Far across the bay, a palate of pink cloud with the most exquisite blue-grey shadings mixed together, their distant turbulence frozen while some magical artist tinted the whole with shades of pale crimson and white, so delicately contoured. And toward him came another floating mass with darker grey undertones, like a solid raft bearing warnings of a storm. Or a celestial omen. He breathed deeply.

Finally, blowing his nose on his handkerchief and clearing his throat, he wiped his eyes and his face and got up. He walked back and entered the open doorway.

The table had been cleared, the dishes washed, and Catherine was lighting their whale-oil lamp. She turned as she heard his step.

He stood, awaiting the awful judgement. He had survived so much. Maybe he could even survive this: the loss of his new wife, daughter, everything. He raised his eyes to see her standing before him.

She came across, a picture of warmth and solace, and folded him into her arms. He buried his head on her shoulder as she hugged him, and rocked him, and patted his back, as she had done many times with Mariah. They stayed this way for a long time, until she led him back to the table by the fire.

She rose, and came back with a piggin which she put in front of him. "Rum. We both need a drink."

He looked up at her, sitting opposite. Her voice had been warm, caring, giving, everything a mature wife could ever be. He lifted the piggin, took a swig and handed it back to her.

She took the piggin, and gulped three or four big swallows, after which she broke out in a fit of coughing.

In spite of himself, he laughed. And she laughed, too.

He rose again, went around the table and she got up into his arms. "Oh God, James, that's awful! Why do you men drink it?"

"Well, we don't drink it that way!" He took the piggin and sipped again. "I feel so much better. Why have I kept it secret for so long?"

"Well, James..." She sat down suddenly. "My head is spinning. I'm angry, I'm very angry."

Well of course. "Yes, Catherine, of course. I understand completely. You must —"

"— because you left that poor little baby all winter long with those horrid people. You must go down to Port Daniel and back up that river, and get him at once. You must bring him here so that we can look after him. He is your son. He needs our love. He needs our care. You'll have to go. As soon as you can. I cannot believe you let that poor little baby be brought up by savages!"

James sat stunned. He lifted the piggin and took a big gulp. He brushed aside her prejudice — just her old-fashioned mother talking, and the heat of passion. She'd soon change. Or would she?

"The first thing I have to do is get back to Paspébiac for our canoe."

"No."

He looked up.

"Something else is more important. First..." She nodded at their bed.

Their marriage was consummated more fully than ever before, and afterwards, James slept the sleep of a good and just man.

***

Two days later, James set off by land to retrieve his canoe in Paspébiac. Across the Nouvelle River, he stopped in to thank the Ross family for saving him and his bull calf. He reported that the animal was recovering, and invited them down to see his new house. On approaching Paspébiac, he slowed down. Those dangerous villains could still be lurking. He had to move carefully, checking for ambushes.

When he arrived, he looked down over the *banc* and saw that his canoe was no longer tied up. Stolen! Devastated, he continued, almost not caring, to the Robin's administration office.

Monsieur Huard, the Robin's manager, hailed him as he neared. "James! We are happy to see you. The rumour, she say you are dead, like poor Jean-Pierre."

"Jean-Pierre?" James reached out to shake his hand.

"Oui, oui. L'homme qu'on a trouvé sur la plage. We find him dead on beach. But you are fine, *hein?"*

"Very fine. But I'd be even finer if I had news of those villains —"

"Ah, *les nouvelles?"* M. Huard went on to recount, partly in French and partly in English, that a group of settlers had banded together and went in search of the villains, finding one still out cold. With not enough evidence to link them to the murder, the settlers still made it clear that the scoundrels were not welcome in Paspébiac and put them on the next schooner for Quebec City. Several workers had wanted to dispatch them on the spot.

"Et maintenant, tu es ici, and you are safe. You some kind of hero for beating them, *hein?"*

M. Huard revealed that M. Robin, who knew of James's exploits offering up his life for the Indian Chief at the *Bellerophon* the previous year, had agreed to give

James a barrel of tar as the Robin's contribution for his efforts in dealing with the villains.

James was delighted. But then, disheartened by the theft of his fine canoe, he blurted out, "My canoe..."

"Safe! My men, they put in warehouse. Very fine canoe. I go myself, I look. Very fine."

Once his canoe was back in the water, the Robin's storekeeper sent an assistant to carry down the tar barrel. So James found himself not only with an ox, but with free tar for his new barn and house.

Chapter Twenty-Four

A month later, in spite of Catherine's continued insistence that he go fetch his son, James had not resolved in his mind how to persuade the tribe to let the child come live at Shegouac Brook. The last thing he wanted was any form of confrontation with his former Micmac family. He needed to resolve all that in his mind before allowing himself to voyage back to Port Daniel.

A few days later, James was digging out a spring that he had found in the hill not far behind the house. With its water, he'd gone across to fill Broad's container. The animal's resuscitation had been almost a miracle. Over the past four weeks, the little animal had grown strong. James kept him tethered by the barn so that Broad could forage for food, and drink from the bucket outside his stable door. Though still emaciated, he was growing into a fine young bull calf. James lifted a flask of the same spring water to his mouth and drank. Above, the sky was streaked with all manner of cloud. Crows called raucously from the tops of trees. A robin made itself heard: a thrush-like warble he loved. Not a soul in sight.

Then a cry came from the Hollow.

He leapt up and was shocked to hear another yell. "James! James!" Catherine screamed, and then silence.

He broke into a run. He soon reached the clearing

around his house. No sign of Catherine anywhere. "Catherine!"

He ran to the door quickly, looked in. He came out, ran behind. No sign. Had some villain grabbed her? Was she being raped in the woods? "Catherine!" he yelled again, and stood, listening hard. Silence.

Where was she? Where was Mariah? Frantic, he came to the front of the house and then, out on the bay, saw war canoes.

Oh Lord, a flotilla! Two, three, yes, four loaded canoes heading his way. So where was Catherine?

"Catherine!" She had hidden herself. But Indians would find her in no time.

He ran back and forth, peering into the bushes that lined the foot of the hill. "Catherine, come down," he called again. "Get in the house. We'll barricade ourselves in."

Oh yes? They only had one measly fastener. He'd been meaning to put up a stout wooden bar. But now, anyone could break in.

So what to do? Get upstairs, load his flintlock and sight down through the dormer window? Thoughts of his pure wife made him panic. So many stories: men scalped, women raped — who were they, coming in full regalia? The Iroquois? Had they massacred his tribe? Should he go and negotiate? With no bars on the door, no real means of defending himself, that was the only option. He headed down his trail, pausing halfway to check once again.

Could it be... he peered intently. Was that man in the costume of a Chief in the central canoe his own Chief from Port Daniel? But why so many canoes? Why head so ominously for his own landing at Shegouac Brook? Coming to seize Mariah? Or snatch his wife, to make up for the loss of Little Birch? Crazy ideas lurched about in his brain.

He kept on down the trail — to reconciliation or death, he knew not which. If he greeted them, diverted them, perhaps Catherine could get away.

On the beach, he stopped. In the canoe with the Chief — did that not look like a woman, holding a baby? Not John? He leapt across the shelving of red rock and stood, a solitary figure, waiting.

One after another, the decorated canoes beached. The occupants nimbly leapt out to haul their crafts above the high-tide line.

James signalled with open arms his welcome.

The Chief's canoe drew up, and from the prow Tongue got out.

James's head spun. What on earth? A ceremonial occasion?

His whole family came ashore: Full Moon carrying John, Brightstar, now a fine young lad of twelve, and One Arm, dressed in his best outfit.

James was so pleased he grabbed Full Moon and hugged her, forgetting again that this was not the Indian way. Gravely, he shook hands with One Arm and Tongue; and finally he could not avoid giving Brightstar a big hug too, as though he were still a little lad, embarrassing him no end, though he did giggle with delight. Full Moon gingerly handed him his son, and he looked for a long moment into the sombre little face.

They all gathered round while he made a short speech, welcoming them to his farmland, expressing extreme pleasure at their visit. He handed back his son to Full Moon and started up the trail, waving them onwards.

His first thought was Catherine. She should be there to welcome them, as right and proper and only to be expected. But was she still hiding somewhere, off in the woods? Had she climbed the hill behind the house, carrying Mariah to safety? When he reached the yard in front of the house, he cupped his hands to his mouth and yelled, "Catherine, come down. Our friends have arrived. Come welcome them."

No answer.

What should he do? How far had she gone?

He tried again: "Catherine, come quickly. We need you. Please! Help me greet them!"

Still no answer.

The entourage broke out into the flat clearing and gathered silently, staring at this newly finished farmhouse and barn, roofs pitched with tar.

In spite of the natural reticence of the Micmac, he could see their eyes glow with satisfaction. He waved them forward, standing by his open door.

They moved forward, albeit with some awkwardness.

Brightstar, unable to contain his excitement, ran over to Broad and began to pat him. But frightened by the enthusiasm, the calf had pulled back to the length of its tether. And then, James saw their heads turn. He looked round.

There stood Catherine at the edge of his cleared land — the picture of an angel, blonde curls over perfectly formed full features, holding a lovely baby daughter, four months old.

"Catherine," he walked quickly over, "come and meet my former family."

"Why have they come?"

"Who knows? Catherine, please be gracious."

"Of course, James, but I'm nervous..."

He brought her down to meet them. "This is Full Moon. And One Arm. Look, little John." Catherine stared at her new son, stricken by this avalanche of new sensations. "Brightstar, come on over and meet my wife," he called in Micmac.

Shy greetings took place, and then they all began to relax, pointing at the house and talking quietly. James could see they were pleased.

Full Moon came closer to Catherine, interested in how she carried Mariah: a piece of cloth improvised around her, on her back. At that age, John had been securely carried on his cradle board. Full Moon was talking volubly all the time in Micmac, explaining the advantages of a cradle board, clearly worried that Catherine's homemade piece of canvas was not sufficient.

"Hold it, hold it," James said in Micmac to Full Moon, "she doesn't understand."

Catherine gestured gracefully for them to enter her home. Cautiously, they picked their way closer, talking among themselves in low tones, admiring the buildings and land.

James held his door wide and ushered them into his all-purpose room. Leading the Chief to the place of honour before the fireplace, James came and sat beside him on the rough bench. Catherine approached, full of conflicting emotions, though her fear had dissipated.

The ceremonial pipe was lit with Indian tobacco that the Chief had grown, as Tongue explained. Catherine went over to take another close look at John. Then she noticed Full Moon checking her utensils on the shelves. Gesturing, she explained each one, and how she cooked with them. James guessed she'd give her selected ones later.

Soon Tongue rose, and the gathering fell quiet. Their shaman, the *Buowin,* who had rescued James from his utter despair, had signified that in a dream Little Birch had come, and ordered the band to rethink their decision about John. Magwés had commanded him to send their best scout to Shegouac to investigate John's father and his new wife. The *Buowin* had been so firm and insistent that the Chief had dispatched their foremost scout, who had indeed come and, unnoticed, observed James and Catherine at work. His report had been positive.

The Chief now rose and spoke in Micmac, of which James caught the gist, announcing the tribe's considered decision. They had reached a consensus that John would be safe in the hands of these English settlers. Then Full Moon, with short but touching phrases, handed the year-old baby to James.

"We should take care of him now, Full Moon?" James asked in Micmac, in formal fashion, Catherine at his side.

Full Moon nodded her full accord, and little John for his part looked up and actually smiled. The group re-acted approvingly.

James put John down, now over a year old, so that he could crawl and pull himself up at the bench. He tottered over to the Chief. Smiling, the stately Indian turned him around, and John tottered back to James and reached up to be taken into his arms. Mariah lay quietly in her pine cradle.

Catherine had stoked the fire, got a kettle boiling, and was able to hand around piggins of valuable tea, though some visitors had to share, there not being enough to go round.

During the ensuing encounter, Tongue translated for Catherine their delight at what the young couple had managed to achieve in such a short time. James gave all credit to Catherine's United Empire Loyalist family. He went on to promise that he would bring John back to the encampment and never let him lose touch with his Native roots, of which he should be justly proud. None of them made mention of Little Birch, for the names of the dead were rarely spoken.

When the time came to leave, as they wanted to be back before nightfall, Full Moon picked her grandson up. She hugged him and kissed him and closed her eyes, from which tears began to fall. James glanced at Catherine.

She, too, had tears in her eyes. "Tell her, James, we shall always be grateful." James translated and Catherine went on, "Tell her that I shall look after John as though he were my own. He will be treated as I would treat my firstborn." James translated, though his brimming emotions almost put a stop to his words. "I shall make sure that he grows into a fine young man."

When James had translated this, he saw Full Moon crying and others holding back tears.

Finally, he walked with them down to their canoes, and stood as one stricken, looking out over the blue-grey sea, waving after them until they rounded the last point and disappeared.

Chapter Twenty-Five

On the bay, a single boat approached.

James and Catherine stared anxiously. Two men? Not Micmac. They appeared to be settlers. Arriving from the west, presumably from Paspébiac or New Carlisle.

"I'm going inside," Catherine said firmly.

"They're only settlers. Don't worry, Catherine. I'll go down."

"Be careful, James!"

He picked up his firearm and strode off down the hill. The trail had been purposefully designed so bushes would obscure his movements from the bay. Halfway down, at an opening, he peered again: two oarsmen for sure, in a fairly new boat. With their backs to him as they rowed, they didn't see him until they were close to shore. The man in the stern turned and said something to his companion in the front, who was pulling hard. They both wore heavy jackets.

James waited on the beach till they arrived and then helped them pull the boat up above the high-tide line.

"We seen your building from the bay," said the man, getting out of the stern. "I'm Bill Mann. This here's my brother, Isaac."

"I'm James Alford. You folks in to check out land?"

"Isaac figured there might be a vacant piece hereabouts. I brung yez a letter." Bill reached into his pocket and pulled out a parchment package, sealed with wax. Such was the custom of the Coast to pass on letters like this.

"Lotsa land, lotsa land hereabouts," James said, and looked down at the package.

"Old Garrett gave it to us."

"Good acreage on that other side of the brook, if you want it."

"Thanks," said the man called Isaac. "John Gilchrist claims she's a right pretty spot here." Isaac's bushy beard hid a slightly mean mouth. His heavyset shoulders were stooped; James guessed him to be a carpenter, probably early thirties. His brother Bill seemed somewhat less taciturn.

"If you'd like to come up to the house, my wife will offer you both a cup of hot soup and a slice of bread." James was dying to find out about the letter.

"Thank you kindly." Bill looked over at his brother getting his rucksack out of the boat.

"We'll just take a look-see first," Isaac muttered. "Thank ye, but we must get back afore nightfall."

James watched the two of them take their tools, an axe and a saw, and splash across the brook. Isaac turned. "Ya say this here waste land's not occupied?"

"That's right," replied James.

"This here brook got any name?"

"The Micmac call it Shegouac."

"Shegouac? Thanks."

"Planning on staying?"

"Just for the day, maybe," said Bill.

"Good flat land up there," James called after them.

Isaac had the grace to turn and wave before he joined

his brother scrambling up the steep hillside through the bushes.

James hurried up his path to report on the newcomers and read his letter. He was not sure if he liked the demeanour of the person who might end up being his neighbour. But then, any man was better than none. Their clothes and appearance gave them a look of substance; Catherine might well know them. Well appointed, they would not be an added responsibility this winter.

After James told Catherine about the Manns, he handed her the opened letter, eyes glowing.

She looked down. "From your mother?"

James nodded. "You can read it if you like."

"James you know I am not able to." She blushed. "You read it out loud."

James frowned. "Your parents didn't school you?"

She shook her head. "Now go on, read it." She added, "No need for extravagances like reading. What is there for me to read anyway?"

"Letters." Gingerly he spread the parchment out on the table.

My dearest son, he began, trying to hide his intense excitement, *I am sending this short note to let you know I'm in good health and looking forward to the trip next summer, although the thought of a passage over the Atlantic fills me with dread. We hear about so many good people coming to their end, their bodies consigned to the deep.*

I must now inform you of rather sad news. Your great ship, the Bellerophon, *has been taken out of commission in the Port of London, and made into a floating prison.*

After its many great deeds, how dreadful for the Admiralty to consign it to such a fate. I shall try to find out more details.

On a trip to town, Goodman the butler was kind enough to enquire into sailings. I shall take a ship from Liverpool, our closest port. So before long, and certainly after the winter, I shall be with you.

I cannot wait to meet your new wife and her family, and especially, to help look after your children.

Your loving mother.

"Welcome news indeed!" Catherine exclaimed. "You must reply at once. The sooner she gets here the better. Mariah will be a year old, and John two. What with all the work, the chickens and bull to feed," James looked up, "and so many vegetables and jams to put up for the winter, I'd welcome another pair of hands."

"I'll write to her immediately. Isaac and his brother can take the letter back to New Carlisle today. And your father, Catherine, will help with the next schooner."

***

Late in the summer, James had been fashioning a large safety bar across the front door at last when out the door he saw two men arriving. The first wore a bushy beard and a floppy hat under which James saw handsome, if somewhat ravaged, features.

"Hello there. I'm Samuel Allen. This fella here's John Rafter."

"Pleased to meet you both." James went forward to shake hands. John, younger than Sam, had a quick and ready smile. Built like fence wire, he was all muscle and clearly used to working hard.

"Sam is getting to be one of the family, so he asked me along."

"This is my wife Catherine, old Will Garrett's daughter. I guess you know them? Come in, come in."

They appeared wet and weary, having rowed all day. "Us saw your house from the bay," Sam said. "Mighty fine building."

Catherine took their wet coats. "I do remember you, Mr. Rafter. You're a good friend of my brothers."

"John and Will? That I am, ma'am."

"John here's involved in shipbuilding, too," Sam said. "His mother and me, we figured I should bring him down for a look-see. Your brook's getting a pile o' mentions as some fine place. But we stopped in every cove first, to look around." Samuel studied the house as they went in. "Well built. Old Gilchrist?"

"Sure was," James replied. "John Gilchrist must have been taken a liking to Shegouac. Told Isaac Mann to come, too."

"Mentioned it to me, too. We work for Isaac sometimes."

"Sam here's a carpenter, builds ships," John volunteered. "Makes the best blocks and tackles."

"Isaac's got a terble pile o' land up round Matapedia. He don't need any here. Anyway, he said this here brook looked good enough for us all, and told me I should row down." He scratched his head. "Seems like Nouvelle River up there, it's got a bunch o' settlers already. Starting both sides, now."

Catherine had hung their heavy outer garments on

pegs near the fire. "You've been looking along the Coast?"

"Not a lot of land free with a nice brook like this between here and Paspébiac," Sam acknowledged.

James motioned for them to sit at the table. "Lots down Pabos way, I believe."

"Anyone live across the brook?" Sam sat down, and John joined him.

"No sir. Isaac Mann came looking. Might have staked out a piece before he went back. But we'd be pleased to have neighbours." James pulled over a chair. "Winters are long. Safety in numbers, I guess." Catherine hurried to offer them warmed-over vegetables and set down cups for their tea.

The Manns, including John's mother, Widow Rafter, and her sons, did end up building a cabin, and came to stay with their children and supplies. The Smiths, prosperous landowners from around New Carlisle, also turned up, and during autumn worked clearing some land further down by the point. But they returned home for the winter.

Chapter Twenty-Six:
Spring 1816

The next year, shirt sleeves rolled up, James worked with his shovel out in the spring sun, digging a trench to divert the fast-running water coming off the hill that threatened the foundations of his new house. Thanks to the good store of moose meat from his first successful hunt, they had weathered the winter. But now, in these early days of May, they were happy to see the snow melting at such a furious rate. Happy, but for the approaching trip to New Carlisle. Spring had come at long last, and with it, the worry of their promised visit to Catherine's family, with the hitherto unknown John, son of a Micmac mother.

What a joy the children had been. Mariah had even begun to stand up on shaky legs. Wobbling on two feet, she'd make a lunge for a chair, falling before she reached it. John, who was by now a handful, would come and tug at her ear. He seemed to delight in her screams, for then he would make a big fuss of kissing her to make it better. James scolded him furiously, but Catherine explained that this was normal behaviour for a two year old. She had been witness to her younger sister Eleanor's babyhood, so knew more or less what to expect.

That morning, with plenty of snow in melting drifts around the barn, James had let Broad out. What fun to see the animal, by now a growing bull, kicking up his heels, frolicking like any youngster. Earlier, James had been worried that he might not last the winter, for he had gotten weaker, and eaten less. James had not really harvested enough fodder last autumn, so perhaps that was just as well. Now, with easy grazing, if it could be called that, on soggy leaves and a few green shoots, Broad soon revived. Three chickens and the rooster were also in bad shape, though they now seemed on the mend, pecking and scratching among the stumps.

James was hoping to hear from his mother about her early arrival, which would take some of the strain off Catherine. Back at the castle, he'd seen his mother work wonders with the young ones, whom she loved to care for when she had the chance. The sooner she got here, the better.

Soon, they'd be planting again. Catherine had been careful to cut the eyes out of all their cooking potatoes, and to save some dry corn for seed. Last autumn she had identified wild gooseberry bushes in the Hollow, as well as wild strawberries and raspberry canes around the cliffs. Highbush cranberries grew in profusion on the hill, and they intended to transplant some to begin their own garden nearer the house.

James was just standing up to survey the results of his digging when Catherine came out to announce noon dinner.

"Well done, James!"

He shook his head at the trench. "Who dreamed the spring run off would produce such a torrent of water?"

Catherine ignored his remark. "And when are you planning our trip to New Carlisle?"

"Pretty soon, I guess. How do you think they're going to react?"

"James, you've asked me that so many times, I for one will be glad when the trip is over."

"You still haven't said anything."

"I haven't said anything because, as you know so well, I am not one bit optimistic."

So there it was. Neither of them was looking forward to going. But go they would, and soon.

***

The spring wind had an icy nip to it, although the sun was doing its best to warm the couple as their canoe sped through the grey, beating waves. In the stern James stroked rhythmically; in front, Catherine was resting between bouts of paddling. The two children, Mariah and John, were heavily bundled up between them in the centre. The rocking of the canoe had lulled Mariah into a doze, while John, having been severely warned, sat well-behaved, playing with a carved wooden horse his father had made.

Overhead, the sun was smiling down through a blue heaven, circled on the horizon by the ever-present Gaspé landscape of clouds. To the east, faint high wisps of cirrus floated onward. And on the western horizon, large rolling bundles of thunderclouds advanced, about to vanquish the clear arc of blue and spread perhaps life-giving rain on the land and water.

The burgeoning waves made James turn his attention to getting safely through. "Catherine, if you're up to it, you should have another go at paddling. It's blowing up."

Catherine took up the paddle and set to work. The seas had become choppy, and the canoe started to buck. A wave splashed over the gunnel and struck young John across the face. He turned to his daddy, and made a face as if to cry. His dignity had been hurt.

"It's okay, Johnnie, it's only water, it'll dry. That's the fun of canoeing — you get real water thrown at you! Like riding a horse. You'd like to ride a horse, wouldn't you?"

John nodded and went back to his toy.

With all his attention on canoeing and seamanship, James found the time passed quickly and before long, they headed in to the floating jetty at New Carlisle. Catherine leaned forward to fend them off as the canoe came alongside; James grasped one rope and held onto it. "You first, Catherine." She clambered out and took the ropes, tying both to stanchions.

During the winter there had been little opportunity to communicate with the family. In January a lone *coureur de bois* passed from Pabos on snowshoes and stayed for a couple of meals and a night's rest. He had taken a letter with their news to the Garretts, not mentioning the new family member. Another time, a settler driving a sleigh over the ice had called in and dropped off the Garretts' reply, accepting gratefully a noonday meal from Catherine. During the winter the bay froze a good way out, but horses were a rarity; most work on the Gaspé Coast was done by oxen.

James was hoping that the Garretts' likely happiness at seeing them now might overwhelm any misgivings. And so now, full of anticipation mixed with real concern, they knocked at the door and swept in on a gust of icy spring wind.

"Well, well, the long-lost new parents! Come in, come in," William Sr.'s booming voice proclaimed in his North Country accent. "We've waited all winter — by gu'm, who the devil is that?"

He looked at Catherine who was unwrapping John. She didn't meet her father's eye, she just set John down. Eleanor went straight to Mariah and hoisted her up. "Well, aren't you a lovely little girl!" She turned to Catherine. "She looks so well, I just don't —"

"— don't know how we did it out there, you were going to say, Mother?"

"No no, hush child. Look William, our first grand-child." She kissed Mariah and gave her a hug, before putting her down again.

William affected a smile, keeping an eye on the toddler, John. James occupied himself with taking off his coat.

Eleanor's motherly instincts came to the fore. She lifted the two-year-old lad. "Well, look at you! You're a fine young man! And who do you belong to?"

"He's an orphan," Catherine stammered. How else, thought James, could she deal with it?

"An orphan? What kind of an orphan did you find in the midst of all that waste land?"

"Well, not exactly an orphan," Catherine ventured.

James had remained silent. It was her family, and she'd best deal with them herself.

Eleanor handed John to him. "Whatever possessed you to take in an orphan, my child? Don't you have enough trouble feeding three mouths?"

"Not really," Catherine replied.

James pitched in. "We managed fairly well, all things

considered. I won't deny it's been hard. But I shot a moose in January, we fished trout, and Catherine has been the most wonderful wife, putting up so many wild vegetables and —"

"Wonderful wife? I'd say! Catherine, are you daft?" William grunted. "What in hell d'ya think yer up to, adding another mouth to feed?" His black eyebrows furled down over his eyes and his mouth twisted into a grimace.

"James has been a wonderful father, too," Catherine said. "We haven't been even close to starvation. And it's only our first winter. We'll get better and better at it. We're planting all sorts of seeds, and we've gotten a good bit of land cleared. You must come and see us." She straightened. "So one small tummy did not overburden us. You'll see, Johnnie is a real delight." She swept over to pick up her stepson and gave him a big hug and kiss.

"John, is it?" Eleanor said. "And so John, where do you come from? What indeed is your lineage?"

James and Catherine traded looks. "Why don't we go into all that," James said, "after Catherine and the children have eaten. It has been a long canoe trip, and a cold one." Mrs. Garrett immediately dropped her confrontational attitude and bustled about, getting food ready. William shook his head and limped over to his favourite chair.

Young John sat staring in guarded astonishment at the strangers. He struggled to his little feet and clambered across the floor to reach for his grandfather's pipe on the windowsill. William Sr., without appearing too brusque, pushed him aside. "Eleanor, take the child, will you?"

"Come, Johnnie," James picked up his son, "come see

the fire. I'm adding wood. Would you like to add some?"

John went to the woodpile and grappled with a log. He managed to stagger with it toward the fire, but tripped and fell, the wood striking him in the chin.

His face broke into a grimace, and James said, "Good boy, John!" He took up his son and, sitting on the bench, checked his chin. "Brave young soldier! You have a big war wound. Like your grandfather."

William almost dropped his pipe, and Eleanor swung her head to look at the child.

The boy's face was tilted up for James to wipe off the blood, and Eleanor stared hard. Catherine asked quickly, "Where are the boys?"

"Doing the chores," William answered, temporarily diverted. "William and John went to the woods again this winter. Nice pile of lumber, they cut." He turned. "Now James, you've not heard our trouble with Jacob Belair? Accused my son of calling him a bloody idiot! Which we all know that he is, o'course. But young Will yelled at him before church the other Sunday. In front of the lot of them. Now Jacob's taken the lad to Court over it. That wife of his, I bet she put him up to it." James shook his head at the sorry tale. "Well, I..." William coughed, "was going to ask you to testify on Will's behalf. Character witness. Told Amasa, you know, the town clerk —"

"Amasa Beebe?"

"That's right, asked him to put off the case till you got here. John Rafter says he'll be glad to testify. Bloody shame, mind you."

"But Will certainly learned his lesson," Mrs. Garrett chimed in.

"Bloody well better learn somm'at. That lad's got to

keep a bridle on that mouth of his. Well, the wood he cut for hisself, he'll have to give that to Belair to settle. Otherwise, it's into prison, I suspect."

"I'll be glad to come, but I don't see how I can help, sir."

"Well, James," William took the pipe out of his mouth, "just make sure you give all your particulars. Y'see, an officer from his Majesty's Royal Navy, well now, among us Loyalists, that's a reliable character witness if ever there was one, a man surely to God to be believed."

James marvelled at how things change. Now a respected officer, and three short years before he'd been a common deserter.

"Just give them all that background, the *Bellerophon* and such like, try to throw in some battles. Bill Crawford's a good sort, I warrant. Fine judge, he's likely to do us a favour and schedule it before he goes off to Gaspé next weekend."

"I'll do anything I can, sir," James said gamely. "We'll stay as long as it takes to accomplish William's acquittal."

"Oh my dears," Eleanor said, "you must stay, yes. I've got to get to know my granddaughter."

"And John," Catherine said firmly.

"Oh yes, of course, John. But Catherine dear, you're not thinking of keeping it?"

"*It*, mother? *It* is called John. I'll be obliged if you treat him as your very own grandchild."

Eleanor looked shocked.

James glanced at Catherine: her mettle was showing at last. Now, watch the fireworks! No one in the world could stand up to his wife when she got her mind set.

"My own grandchild?" Eleanor retorted sharply. "Whatever do you mean, Catherine?"

"Exactly what I said!" Catherine replied.

"Hold on, hold on, you'll not speak to your mother like that in my house!" William struggled to his feet.

"You stay out of this, William," barked Eleanor.

Catherine went on, "If my mother won't be civil in this house to her own grandson, then we shall not stay in it one day longer!" James saw his wife rising fully into the fray at last. But oh dear, the sparks had started to fly.

"Catherine," Eleanor said, "are you trying to tell us you intend to keep this orphan as if it were your own?"

Catherine rose. "Well, you might as well know all about it. But it must not go any further."

Her parents waited expectantly.

"That is James's child, which he fathered with a Micmac woman."

James did not want to look up.

Catherine's parents froze as if struck by lightning.

Catherine went on evenly, "I've promised him — on my life and that of Mariah — that I shall care for John as if he were my own!" Catherine's eyes flashed as she scooped up John and tore upstairs. James saw she might give herself up to tears any second.

The reaction could not have been more explosive had she detonated a forty-eight pounder right there in the room. James went quickly to Mariah and picked her up.

"Young man!" William shouted, "Is there any single grain of truth in what she said?"

"Every word, on my honour, sir." As James stood, he felt himself relax. The secret was at last out, for better or for worse. "The sooner you both come to terms with this, the sooner you will get your daughter — and your granddaughter and your son-in-law, and your new grandson — back into the fold."

Eleanor collapsed in tears on the window bench, and William roared, "A savage for a grandson? Never!"

Chapter Twenty-Seven

What was the wind doing? Not another storm? The two children were asleep and so was Catherine. James rolled out of bed, crept carefully to the dormer window installed the previous autumn, and looked out. Snow!

Not in July! Not again!

His shoulders slumped. The rift with Catherine's parents had given them both heavy hearts, and the weather matched their mood. He crept across the freezing room and padded down the stairs. Shivering, he crossed to the open fire, fed some birchbark onto the embers, and blew on it. When it caught, he fed it twigs and added dry wood. Then he leaned back against the stone fireplace he had recently built. What was happening to their summer? The spring had begun badly with that unfortunate reception from the Garretts.

"It was, more or less, what I had expected," Catherine had said on their return. "But James, they'll come around sometime."

"What about your brothers?"

"Young Joseph is swayed by John, who's on our side. But Will is not an easy person, although he's indebted to you for defending him in that lawsuit."

"The lawsuit? It was a joke. The judge, Mr. Crawford, thought the whole thing a ridiculous waste of time.

He ruled that five measures of board be given to Jacob, and it was over in a matter of minutes."

"Will becomes more difficult the older he gets."

James nodded. "I still think he may end up siding with your parents."

Catherine paused, a hint of sadness in her eyes. "But for the moment, James, we have more than enough to do than waste our time worrying about my prejudiced parents."

And so they had continued working all spring, full of optimism. The first warm day, they had planted seeds started inside the house in the southern windows.

The first disappointment had come in early June. All of May they had worked hard preparing more land for planting, having first shored up the house foundations against the usual spring flooding. And then, a freak snowfall had killed every shoot.

Nothing for it but plant again. He and Catherine put in the few seeds they had left: the rest of the seed potatoes, some corn, and leftover wheat. No harvest without planting, and no food for the winter without a harvest. At the end of June, thankfully the weather had turned a bit warmer: most of the shoots had taken and were beginning to thrive. And now this unaccountable July snowstorm.

No wonder Isaac Mann had gone off to New Carlisle last week; he had a good bit of land up near Restigouche anyway. Before leaving for good, Isaac had made a quick trip to New Carlisle for news. Not good. Snow had fallen across Lower Canada; Quebec City had been blanketed, and a schooner Captain told them all along the Coast had suffered even worse. James felt sure they'd lose the

Smiths, too. Vid Smith had a fine farm up toward New Carlisle, and although David his son was doing well down here and wanted to make a go of it, they might not last this out. That left Samuel Allen and his flock. He hoped they'd stay.

But then, what about him and Catherine? With the Garretts' reaction to his half-Micmac son, returning would not be possible. Not that he wanted to.

To make matters worse, the anticipated letter from his mother had reached them. She planned on coming as invited. How would he feed her this next winter, as well as Catherine and the two children? Last summer when he had written her, he'd had no idea the weather would foreclose on all their dreams. Was he bringing her over here just to starve to death?

Don't think about that, he sternly commanded. Focus on what must be done now. That's always been your motto: deal with the present, and let the future fall where it may. But how to deal with a snowstorm in July?

***

Smash! Crash! Over and over again, James slammed the precious wooden bucket against the rocks. It flew into pieces. He grabbed up one of the staves and smashed it hard, beating and beating. Beside him, Broad turned his head, thrust his ears forward, stared with large brown eyes. James kept cursing and beating until he could beat no more. Then he turned and sat on a log, his head in his hands. He wished he were twelve years old again so that he could cry out loud. But tears would not come.

The darned buckets had come loose so many times on

the walk up the hill. He had tried various ways to fasten them to Broad's back so that they would not spill. He'd thought he had finally beaten the problem. And for a week it had worked. But now, one had slipped and spilled all the brook water. He'd have to go back down. So many things. So much going wrong. More than a man could stand.

Look. There, beside the trail, the snow still lay where it had fallen two days ago, not even melting. And here it was August! Snow in June and July had been bad enough. But now, something was truly amiss — the year with no summer.

Young Broad stood obedient and silent, facing up the hill. Overwhelmed with hopelessness, James despaired of finding enough food for the little bull this winter. Never mind Broad, how would they survive themselves? Had he brought two children into the world only to suffer a lingering starvation?

Day after day this summer, he and Catherine had arisen and had been forced to dress warmly to do a day's work. Time after time, they had tried to nourish a few small plants. And time after time, with the temperature so low, most plants had withered — even the stoutest would produce little corn; few potatoes of decent size lurked in the rich soil. Would the trout in the brook be fat and sleek this autumn, as in other years? Of course not. Even the small game, on which he relied for trapping, would diminish as their habitat was unable to replenish itself. The sun daily declined to show its face, hiding behind a cloak of continuous cloud. And what a curious colour in the sky: dark red sunsets and, all day long, a murky grey-brown pall hanging over the landscape.

The talk, up and down the Coast, was how to face this winter. What could James feed the chickens? They'd all have to be eaten eventually. Devastation everywhere.

Nor was the news from Quebec City good. This snow had struck the capital in all its fury, smothering buildings, outlying gardens, and fields as well. The government would surely have too many problems of its own to bear in mind this distant Coast. Schooners had reported in Paspébiac that city markets carried far less produce than normal. Last week, James had trudged up the now familiar path to Nouvelle and spent the afternoon discussing matters with John Ross. He was even more worried, with eleven mouths to feed. Everyone agreed this had never happened before.

James happened to turn his head and see, on the brow of the hill, the figure of Catherine. She started down the trail.

"I'm sorry," James said simply. He waved his hand at the smashed bucket.

"I understand, my dearest. I understand very well." She nodded to herself. "You know, James, these last three or four weeks, I have been speaking to you roughly, as no wife should. But 'twas only the frustration talking."

James sighed. "And I thought, myself, I could be strong for both of us." He shook his head. "I've lost the will to go on." He let his head slump into his hands.

Catherine reached out and touched him. "It will pass, James. It will pass." He felt her bend and kiss him on the head.

"It's all very well to say that, but when there's nothing to eat, how shall we go on?"

"I have no answer. But I do believe that we must."

James gestured at the dirty, decaying drifts still lying in hollows around. "Snow. In August. Am I seeing things?"

The happiness bird, his companion at the cabin, called from a nearby tree. Yes, in the past it had seemed like a promise, but now James wasn't so sure. But with Catherine's motherly comfort, James found himself feeling a bit better. He surveyed the remains of the bucket he had carefully crafted over two days, now a victim of his tantrum.

"I'd better hold myself in check, or I'll be spending all my time making new implements!" An odd smile grew on his lips and he reached over and kissed his wife on the cheek. "You are the best. If any man can look after you this winter, it will be me. That cloud of despair, which clung to me all that spring before we met? I did survive it. And look what came next — you, the one treasure of my life. Where the next will be found, I know not, but find it we shall."

"The treasure, my dear James, is in your own heart. You will discover strengths that you never even knew existed. And that strength will carry me, and our two children, and dear Broad," she slapped at the ox and he swished his tail, "and all of us will survive."

"By the grace of God, Catherine, yes, survive we must."

***

James heaved hard, dug his feet into the pebbled beach, and pushed out the rowboat. The Allens were leaving, bent on their own survival. Samuel had gathered his family, given James and Catherine some of the stores they had gathered through the summer, not very much, but welcome indeed.

Samuel had hurt his leg rescuing a distressed boat last winter, and now had two ulcers, one above and one below the knee. Some midwife in New Carlisle might help, or perhaps the doctor would return for one last visit. Catherine had come down to the beach with the children to see the Allens off.

"As you know, I'm expecting my mother," called James.

"I'll keep my eye on any schooner that arrives from the Old Country," replied Samuel as the boat drew out of earshot.

"We're sorry to see you go," James called, echoed by Catherine.

"We'll be back in spring, no fear." Samuel dug in his oars. His three children were seated in the stern, with Widow Rafter in the prow facing the bay. They turned and waved. The two families had shared many a good time over the summer, even in the midst of their general despair. With a tot of rum and a draft of good friendship, they had seen their way to merriment in the midst of gloom, and it was with sinking heart that James watched them move off over the waves. All their hoped-for neighbours had dispersed: the Smiths, David Senior and Junior, were going back to their original farm; Isaac Mann too — everyone seemed to think that survival in New Carlisle might be a better option than Shegouac, so aptly named by the Micmac: Nothing There.

The family made their way up the hill, as though it were the Mount of Desolation. So little to eat, so little harvested, and nothing to help them understand how to survive that cruel winter rapidly approaching.

Chapter Twenty-Eight

Bundled up against the cold, James had spent a weary morning out with his shovel looking for roots, and searching among the bare trees for cattails. Not as tasty as cow-lily roots, these roots could be cooked like potatoes and would provide some nourishment. Catherine dried them under hot ashes and ground them into a kind of flour for cattail bread or soups. He'd taken note of a couple of new red oak trees. The ones closer to home had all been picked over for their acorns, which Catherine duly roasted, ground, and made into a kind of acorn bread.

Worn out, James was walking up the trail from the Hollow carrying his sack of cow-lily roots when Catherine greeted him. She held a battered and folded paper, sealed with wax. "This might be important. One of my father's friends brought it by boat while you were off this morning."

James fingered the heavy parchment, turning it over and over. Must be his mother; though the writing was different. He and Catherine had both been waiting for her. Not a day had gone by when they hadn't questioned why no word had arrived. Of course, the journey might be difficult, and they presumed she may have stopped in Quebec, or Halifax, both places requiring an overland excursion.

Summoning all his strength, he hurried up into the house, and sat down to break the seal. Catherine watched as he unfolded the outside paper, which contained the precious letter from his mother inside. And he started to read.

My dearest son,
I cannot believe what has been happening on board. But I am determined to tell you everything, until I can write no more. First let me tell —

James stopped, put the letter down, and gazed into space. *Until I can write no more.* What could that mean?

He had better involve Catherine. "Let me read you the first paragraph."

James read the words slowly, ending with *until I can write no more.* He looked across at Catherine and she dropped her eyes.

"Go on, James," she said gently.

First, let me tell you how overjoyed I was to get your letters. They filled me with such hope. I read them to some of the staff at Raby Castle, who ended up being very helpful with my preparations to leave. As you may know, this trip has been long in the planning. And but for my present unfortunate predicament (which I shall explain below) it has turned out to be everything, and more, that I could ever have hoped for.

James paused, and glanced over at Catherine. She did not meet his eyes, but sat motionless, like a statue. Did she know what was coming?

James went on reading.

You will be pleased to know that I came into an inheritance which permitted me to buy suitable clothes for the voyage and a good ticket on the schooner.

You would not believe what fine clothes and the rattle of coins in one's purse can do for a woman of my age. I have never before experienced such attention. When I arrived in Liverpool for my departure, I stayed at good accommodations, and even treated myself to a hairdresser. I find it alarming, even so, to see how appearances count. Not so, I gather, in your part of the world. You must tell your dear wife how lucky she is to avoid such prejudice.

I did spend two days seeing around Liverpool, sparing no expense. Such a lovely time! You will see how this inheritance, my dearest son, has been very well spent, considering the state I find myself in now. Although I worried you might have needed it, I believe you are in good enough circumstances to be happy with how my last days were spent.

James paused again. This time Catherine reached across and put her hand on his. He dropped his eyes, hoping for the best, but fearing what lay in the pages beneath.

First, let me say that only now do I fully understand what you must have gone through in the British Navy. How do those sailors, poor things, manage to climb such horribly high masts, furling and unfurling the topmost sails so very high in the air? When I boarded my ship, full of hope, it looked quite large, but now in the midst of these enormous waves, I feel I am in one of the cork boats you used to launch on Belham stream near the Castle, when you were eight years old.

Thank the Lord I am not among the lower classes, where the poor dears huddle in the bowels of the ship, vomiting. So terrible for them, and it makes me careful not to list my own limited sorrows here. Not a day goes by but another body is wrapped in canvas and committed to the deep and the arms of our dear Lord Jesus.

When I came on board, I was that evening introduced in the mess, as it is apparently called, to a fine gentleman who also hails from the North Country. A widower, he was coming to see his son, just as I was coming to see you. His son has also done well, too, opening a branch of his father's trade in Montreal. This ship is ending its voyage in Montreal, where he would have disembarked.

James paused, then went on, *In the few short days before we dropped anchor in the Canary Islands, we got to know each other quite well. I felt the contact would be useful for you in the New World, for he was a man of substance, and I'm sure his son must be also.*

"Was?" James again looked over at Catherine.

We talked of many things, and spent time on the deck in the blowing wind, for at first the ship sailed under clear blue skies. Our course was directed toward the Caribbean Sea, which I discovered lies to the south of those new United States. Although they did break away from the King, that war between us is over and so we were due to call first at Boston, then proceed to Quebec, where I intended to disembark. I am told it is close enough to the Gaspé Coast.

Tenerife in the Canaries was extraordinary. I don't think I have ever felt in Northumberland such warm weather. Glorious days we spent, just the two of us, John Westberry and I, such a gallant gentleman, he took me everywhere. I felt young and attractive again. No don't laugh at that, for it would not be too much to admit that these last two weeks, I was very, very happy.

Dear James, our last day in Tenerife, my John complained of a headache, and the next day ran a high fever. And this is where I must admit that the dreaded typhus raging on the Continent has seized many of our crew and passengers.

James put down the letter, fearing to read on. Catherine squeezed his hand and nudged him. He continued.

It has now taken off the one who has given me such happiness. John Westberry was consigned to the deep yesterday. And, my dearest son, I hesitate to tell you, but I must. It has now taken firm hold of your unworthy mother.

James could read no more. He put down the letter, and bowed his head. Catherine rose, went to sit and put a strong comforting arm around him, holding him tightly.

They stayed that way for a while, but then James, wanting the whole truth, picked up the letter and continued.

Dear James, do you remember that nobleman who took such an interest in you? You were not privy as I was to the fact that he held no great regard for our master, the Earl, but kept coming for those grouse shoots only to see you. After you left, his visits became fewer, and soon stopped altogether. Well you might ask, why was this?

First, I have to tell you that he too has gone into the arms of His Maker — felled by some stroke which turned him at first into an invalid. When he passed on a year ago, he sent me an envelope in which I found the significant sum which permitted all this. He had fallen on hard times and part of his estate went for sale, which caused him a good deal of grief. His present wife had little idea of finance, and went through everything he owned. He never spoke ill of her, but led me to believe that she was not the woman for him. And you know how things are over here. He had to make the best of it. I am afraid her spendthrift ways were the finish of him.

This is now the third day since my fever began and it has been getting worse. This has been written in fits and starts, between headaches and chills, and aching bones. But if I do nothing else, I must finish.

I had been intending when I arrived to take all the time in the world to explain the circumstances of your birth. You have been such a good son, never asking about that. Letters are such a dreadful means of communicating anything but the most superficial of news. But I must continue.

You see, my first service was in the employ of this Marquis who came to visit you. It was plain even then that his wife was truly a monster. Their marriage had been arranged by their families. He saw that I alone understood this, and for four wonderful years, he would come alone from London to his estate where I worked and we were able to share a good deal. In the end, I produced for him a son and heir. But an heir that could not, given the circumstances, inherit what was rightly his. And so it was felt for all our sakes, I should take you with me to another position, one that he kindly acquired for me as Under-Cook at Raby Castle.

And that, my dear Thomas — no I must call you James now — that is the circumstances of your birth. I only wish I could have told you all this in person. But I'm afraid...

<u>The next day</u>. I fear I shall not live to see the end of the morrow. I am promised a fine burial, as accorded one in my assumed position. I have also taken what little I did manage to save and given it to the Captain, who assures me, under oath, that this precious letter with its contents will be safely delivered in your hands.

I shall not speak of my physical woes. Know only that these last few months — believing that once again I would be with you and your precious wife, and having lived for a short time like a real lady — have been among the happiest in my life. Except for the years I was often in the arms of your father.

I send my love to your beautiful wife, and to your offspring.

I wish it had been otherw —

A scrawl of the pen across the paper ended the missive.

James clenched his eyes shut and screwed his hands into a fist. After a moment, tears fell on the wooden planks of the table. Catherine's arms around him only made the pain worse. At last, he turned his head into her shoulder and she held him as she would a baby.

After a time he took the letter, sat up stiffly, and read it once again right through, with his heart like a stone that continued to sink through untold depths.

And then he took the papers, having first ascertained that none of the sterling notes referred to by his mother were enclosed. Well, you could hardly blame the folks through whose many hands this must have passed, in times like these. Nothing he could do now. He crossed to the fire, knelt, and consigned the letter to the flames that licked and flickered over the now dying embers.

Then he rose. He turned to Catherine, who wiped away her own tears. "We shall speak of this no more."

"No more," she promised. "No one need know of your unfortunate circumstances. Any more than they need know of John's parentage."

And so, James tried to ready himself for trying times, finding money and food for the long and lonely winter ahead.

Chapter Twenty-Nine

Could it get any worse? James wondered. Here he was, lying by the fire, an invalid. How many times had he gone over his actions in helping Amos Hall? Why had he tried to be a hero and lift that barrel of flour off his cart all by himself? Had he been trying to show off? Or just trying to get the job done quickly? He'd been so grateful to old Amos for having offered him a few days' work so that he could buy food. At any rate, he'd felt his back snap, and down he went. They even had to bring him home by sleigh over the bay ice.

He sat up and turned his back to the fire, hoping the muscles and fibres might absorb the heat, relaxing them. He had taken to doing this the last few days, and found it helped. Catherine had suggested alternating that with snow from outside packed into a canvas pouch, which he lay on. Heat and cold. His back might even be getting better. He would soon be able to walk up and down stairs, although when he tried to begin his winter chores, Catherine prevented him.

So for the moment, he sat, inactive, a burden to Catherine, who had all the care of their two children, as well as Broad and the chickens. Thank heaven his mother was not here to feed as well; he was even grateful she had gone on to other realms above, her lifelong work at the castle finished. No more drudgery, no more anxiety about her son in far-off lands. Her letter with its description of those last happy days with a new suitor and sufficient funds to enjoy Liverpool and get a decent passage on the ship, helped assuage his grief. Though he still wondered at the curious workings of the Lord who was bringing this suffering upon him now.

Catherine had become adept at snowshoeing, fetching supplies from their lower cabin, and foraging among the snowy woods for bark to make soups, digging out roots, anything to supplement their meagre supplies. They still had a few potatoes, some of John Ross's present of crushed oats for morning porridge, but the grain was gone. Flour was much too expensive, over four shillings a barrel. Catherine had even raided the store of mildewed oats they intended for Broad. Would their bull end up being eaten too? Any hope of James clearing his land, of becoming a real farmer, was fast disappearing. He even found himself dwelling on the fate of the *Bellerophon*. Imagine, his once proud ship, home for many victorious years, now sunk to the level of a prison hulk! Depression's black cloud descended again.

Starvation faced them. Before his back went out, he had managed to procure a few supplies in New Carlisle but they would be gone soon too. What would February bring? And March? And April? His beautiful farm, his dreams, his land, all abandoned, in ruins. Just waiting for some other hardy settler to come and seize it. But no settler, no matter how hardy, was escaping this peril. The whole Coast, in fact the country itself, was in peril. The year of no summer. 1816.

He remembered when he had gone off to hunt moose last winter, how Catherine had been more worried than usual. What if he were hurt, how would she keep the land? What were the laws of succession? Would she have a home? "James, we must get our land deeded somehow. I'm worried about it."

"But you're a beautiful woman — if anything happened to me, you'd have suitors galore. No fear for the future. You'll be besieged."

"James, stop that talk. I want you; I want no other." She closed her eyes and a tear fell to the table.

James reached out to hold her hand tightly. "Catherine, I told you my dream, my vision: we will live to a ripe old age. I saw both of us. I am sure it was from the Lord Above — vouchsafing to us, if we continue in His ways, a fine future with all our children. Now let's have no more black thoughts."

But black thoughts he most certainly was having, as he gave himself up to despair.

Later that afternoon, Catherine blew in out of the snow, her pale cheeks rosy with frost, her eyes flashing, her voice pitched high from the cold. "We have a visitor! Grey horse and sleigh. They're trying to make it up the hill from the brook. Must have come over the ice. Could be that friend of yours from Nouvelle."

She threw off her coat, looking peaked, but lovely as ever, James thought, and then returned to the door to usher in — sure enough — John Ross, and with him his son.

"Come in, come in!" James managed to rise to his feet. "Well, I didn't know you were one of the lucky ones with a horse!"

John Ross entered, a big tall man, accustomed to winter obviously, with a huge bearskin coat. "Got him as a colt, in trade. Yessir, real useful. This here's my eldest bye, John." About twenty, the lad was not as tall as his father but with the same long, thin face, short black eyebrows and mouth in a straight line. His hair was close cropped under the cap, which he took off on entering.

"Came down over the ice?" James asked.

John nodded. "Never seen so much this early," John said. "Lots of fellas come past me on the ice. Not often I seen that."

"More and more of us," James agreed, sitting to lessen the pain. "I couldn't believe the number of settlers in East Nouvelle. So the road from Paspébiac to the river is better."

"This side of the river now, too. The McCraes, old Farquhar specially, they've been settled there a good while. And his son Duncan."

"Well, the march of progress," responded James. "If the weather ever turned back to its bountiful self, more'd be coming, too." He resolved, later this spring, God willing, to run a real clear line delineating his property. With Catherine's carping the last little while, he'd become as wary as she of someone coming after their land. "Any talk of a land commission yet, John?"

"Been some. But nawthin' this winter, us all so close to starvation. No point in getting land if you're going to die on it."

"And you, what about you, John?" Catherine asked gently.

"Terble hard, ma'am, with a big family. Crops never grew." He and his son accepted the cups of watery soup offered by Catherine.

James sipped in silence, shifting uneasily to lessen his

pain. "So what brings you here, to our homestead, John?"

John sipped his soup. "Well, there's talk of a pile of people gathered up in Carlisle at the courthouse..."

"Oh yes?"

"Ship from Quebec docked last week. Some fellas got a pile of money unloading it. Stored it all in the courthouse."

"Stored what?"

"Flour, they say. Barrels of flour."

James's eyes widened. "A new supply of flour? From where?"

"Must be Quebec," young John said.

"Talk is," John Ross went on, "we only got to go and make a petition."

James had heard that through the autumn, settlers on the Coast had been complaining, even agitating, about the inactivity from the government. Could this now be producing results?

John Ross shrugged. "I reckon we better go and if there's enough to go round, we'll be sure t'get some." He glanced up at Catherine, who had been standing still, almost frozen, at this exciting news. "So I came to get yez. Got the sleigh outside. We'll get us some barrels of flour, and I'll bring yez back down."

Catherine gave James the hug of his life as he rose unsteadily. He too felt his despair evaporating. They'd make it through, yes, with flour and potatoes, they would make it through.

***

With the supplies they had petitioned for and gotten,

they had weathered that endless winter. And now, two years later, James was focussed on keeping his land. Last summer he had run a really good line, along the cliffs for five acres, and then run straight back for about a mile. It covered about two hundred acres.

Now he was building a better roadway up from the Hollow for the sleighs and carts that seemed to be coming more frequently. Catherine was clearing stones off the track and lining them along the sides. Little John had a small bucket and was helping fill in the ruts while Mariah was pottering happily, stooping from time to time to pick up bugs she would put in her mouth. Oh well, thought James, she'll likely eat a peck of those before she dies.

From above, he heard a loud bawl from Broad. He glanced up, but paid no further attention. Until an answering bawl came from another ox.

James straightened. So did Catherine. They looked at each other. Broad began a full bawling welcome. James frowned, dropped his shovel, and walked over to investigate. He rounded the house, and what should he see break through the woods to the west but an oxcart loaded with a family.

The entourage bumped across the foot of his property down by the cliffs, and stopped. A man about his own age jumped off the cart and came across.

"You must be James Alford? I'm James too. Come meet my wife, Mary Nielsen." James walked across to greet her and help her down, as the newcomer dealt with his children. "This big girl here is Elizabeth." James smiled at the pretty youngster, about five years old. "And that there's Sarah, and this here baby is Henriette. I see yez got some kinda slope down into the Hollow there." James Nielsen pointed to where his cart was heading.

"Just fixing up a road now. How far you going?"

"This is it, I guess," Nielsen said. "Mary's relatives on the other side of the brook, they suggested there might be another piece of land we could grab a hold of. This spring looked good, best ever. So come this July, we decided to make a try."

"Stuff sure has been growing," James agreed. He led them up toward the house. "See my potatoes? Up on top of the hill I've started wheat. Showing not too badly. Terrible long time to clear a patch of land, I'm learning."

"I see your corn comin'. Looks like you'll have a good year."

James was still trying to place the stranger and figure out which of his neighbours he was related to.

By now Catherine had come up the hill with her two children: Mariah, who always asked to be carried, now happily ran along ahead of her mother, following John, who pulled up short to stare in wonder at the impressive ox with its handsome, though cobbled together, cart behind.

"And this is Catherine," James said. "My children, John here, and Mariah. I guess maybe you'd better all come inside. Catherine, think we could rustle up some supper?"

James Nielsen introduced his family and they accepted her invitation to walk in, admiring the house which they were surprised to see this far from Carlisle. "I'm just making up a stew, if you give us a bit of time."

"Let me give you a hand, Catherine," Mary said. "I've brought some provisions. We'll let the men gossip."

The two men walked over to the beach trail. "First thing I intend," Nielsen volunteered, "after we get somewhere to live, is cut a decent trail back through them woods." He jerked his thumb towards the Nouvelle River. "Took all day just to get them last four miles. Farquhar McRae warned us. Nice old lady too, Widow Travers, she told us it was nigh impossible to get through. She was right."

"Good idea," James said. "You know, the Allens, Smiths, and that Sam Allen, they all moved back this summer. I reckon they'd be happy to help, if we all took spells. Wouldn't take too long to make us a kind of rough track."

But James could see that an iron-clad deed to his house and land was more urgent than ever. Settlers were beginning to crowd around, grabbing whatever land they could. Before long, he could foresee a dangerous struggle. Who would have thought that, only three short years ago?

***

The Nielsens stayed a couple of weeks, and with the help of the Smiths and Sam Allen, helped James clear and fix the brook trail and on up the other side to the flats beyond the Hollow. And so the summer progressed. The neighbours sometimes got together on weekends. Later, they all pitched in, with Sam Allen's expert direction, to raise James Nielsen a house. He had selected a plot of land near the brook, further back, given him by his relative, Isaac Mann.

One autumn evening, Catherine came down the stairs,

having put the children to bed. She sat beside James as he was carving a doll for Mariah.

"With these new neighbours, and more coming along, we don't have any one piece of paper to show that we own our land, James."

He agreed with her, of course. He had long intended to do something about registering it. But what? So far as he knew, no mechanism existed to safeguard what you had always believed to be rightfully yours. Suppose some highly placed family with no morals just came and seized it? "You know this spring I ran a good clear line on the west there, back for a mile. That's all we need." But was it?

"The Nielsens coming just proves it — we're going to be crowded out." She got her sewing. "By the way, James, when are you going to buy some lambs? We need the wool. I want the children to have pullovers and warm socks next winter. They're growing fast."

James nodded. "Maybe so. I'd been thinking of getting us a cow for milk, too. But maybe sheep first."

"Either way. We could do with butter, and homemade cheese, curds and whey, I remember how my mother —" Catherine stopped, looked down, and changed the subject.

James could see that she was still worried about her family, as was only right and proper. So had he not better tell her the news that the Nielsens brought? "I didn't know if I should tell you, but John and Will are in jail in Quebec."

Catherine dropped her sewing. She looked up in dismay. "In jail? Who told you?"

"The Nielsens. Apparently your father was devastated."

"Well he might be. I am, too!"

"They owed money, I gather. So into debtors' prison they went. Something to do with the building of their ship, I would imagine. John must have been counting on getting some cargo runs to pay for all the fittings. But those companies in Montreal, they slapped them with a court summons."

James had heard that the prison was fairly new, a great square stone building but very dark inside, no windows, one convict per cell. If you were drunk, or penniless, or indeed a woman taken in adultery, in you went with the common criminals; the food was of course atrocious.

She put her sewing on her lap. "What do we do now?"

"I reckon your father, with the right influence, will get them out fast enough. He'll pay their debts, though I bet he'll be angry!"

Catherine smiled. "I bet he will too." Then she dropped her eyes. "I'm sorry, James. But I do miss them all."

***

In the summer of 1819, James came in and closed the door. Catherine was sitting at the table, feeding Mariah and John their breakfasts. They had grown like weeds, and John had even become a bit of a help to his father around the farm.

"Sheep are looking good." James came across to sit and have his morning cup of tea.

"Next it'll be a cow?" Catherine poured some for James and sat down to drink hers.

"Yessir! Going to get us two calves soon." James stirred

some molasses into his hot tea. "Seems there's some sort of commission taking place."

Catherine looked up sharply. "Commission? What sort of commission?"

"Something to do with land, I think. Sam Allen's been telling me."

"Sam Allen?"

"He goes back and forth to Carlisle so often. He's a certified scaler you know."

"So what's this commission about? Must be up to no good."

"Well, you may be right, from all the talk. Those rich fellows up in Quebec and Montreal, they've gotten some pretty big land grants. Two thousand acres, some of them."

"And you think they might be coming down here to take our farm?"

"I didn't say that. I just don't have good feelings when I hear about fellows from the government coming here."

"Where are they going?"

"New Carlisle. They're up there now." James sipped his tea.

Catherine looked up. "Now? James, hadn't you better go?"

"Go where?"

"Don't act silly," Catherine snapped. "To New Carlisle. Find out what's happening."

"Well, that's just what I've been thinking. And you know something, Catherine? Maybe you should come, too." She looked up sharply.

James paused, and then went on. "Do you good. You haven't been up for a long while."

James was only too aware how, over the past couple of years, with the road between here and Nouvelle being open and somewhat travelled, and with the beginnings of a community here in Shegouac, his precious wife still thought about the family she had left behind. Time to do something about it! He was glad the land commission subject was prodding them into action. The time had come.

Catherine rose and put the children's dishes in a tub which she would take outside to wash. "I'll think about it."

As she went to the door, James turned. "No more thinking about it, Catherine. I'm going. And you're coming. We're going together. Tomorrow morning."

"And what do we do about the children? And the animals?"

"James Nielsen told me he'd look after them. The children?" He paused. "We'll bring them, of course." He stood and looked at her. He knew she'd see the resolution in his face. And that, usually, was that!

She turned to go out the door. "All right. I'll start getting us ready."

So now he had two great battles to fight, her family, and winning a deed to his land.

Chapter Thirty

The gentle rocking of the Micmac canoe as James and Catherine headed toward New Carlisle did little to quell his worries. What would the land commission be up to? And how would the Garretts take their arrival? He hoped that by now Eleanor and William Sr. would be regretting their lack of grandchildren. John and Mariah were the only two they had.

As he paddled on, his mind went back over the farm. What a difference Broad had made all winter long, skidding logs. James had cut a good many for floating down his brook, and in spring and summer had traded them for goods, the first one being a spinning wheel for Catherine. No point in having sheep if they weren't going to be able to use the wool. The chickens were multiplying now, lots of eggs. That meant healthy bread. Good cakes. In fact, trading the lumber he cut while clearing his land brought all manner of good things. Nothing like the barter system, he reflected. A shilling could be easily stolen, but try to steal a load of logs! A good way of life.

Nothing James loved more than speeding his canoe with his family through the water. What a great gift it had been! And how he missed his Micmac friends! But he and Catherine had finally agreed that it would be best for young John to continue in the status quo, with Catherine as his only mother and James his father, playing with the children of the white settlers around. Too divisive for him to try to learn Micmac ways just yet. It had been a long process of healing, and he wanted to leave the scars unscratched. And much too hard for Mariah to learn that John was only a half-brother. The main thing now was for John to be accepted by the Garretts. Well, by the end of the day, they would know the answer.

James never ceased to wonder at those great, red cliffs passing. In the winter, he'd marvelled at the huge hanging icicles that now appeared as summer waterfalls. He had discovered — as John Ross's sleigh had sped over the flat, frozen ice – why many winter travellers used that means of transportation. Smooth, no obstacles, and you could, as the saying went, go straight as the crow flies. "You know, I bet one could fish through that ice," James thought to himself. He might try that next winter.

"There she is!" Catherine sighted New Carlisle around the bend in the cliffs. Although she appeared excited, he knew she was worried about the coming confrontation — and the ever-looming possibility of losing their land. So much at stake.

When they reached the floating jetty, who should they see but little Ben, saying good-bye to a Frenchman and putting change in his pocket. With the help of the worker, Ben hefted up the bag of flour, and balanced it on his head as they apparently did in Portugal.

"Ben! What are you up to?"

The lad turned, heaved down the bag, and rushed over. "James! Hello Mrs. Alford." He looked down at the two toddlers, then up at James again. "You fellas been busy, I see."

"That we have," Catherine replied. "How good to see you Ben. I thought you'd be back at the mill."

Ben looked a good deal older: perhaps in his twenties. James resisted hugging him, but he loved the lad and regretted not finding a way to have him work at his own house.

"Oh no, ma'am, the mill shuts in winter."

"But anyway," James asked, "you survived that terrible year of no summer?"

Ben nodded. "Terble hard. A lot of us nearly starved. But they brought Mr. Hobson lots of bread and turnips and potatoes and stuff, for teaching their young 'uns."

"The schoolteacher?" James asked. "Ben Hobson?"

"Yes sir. After you an' me, we did all that studying, well, Mr. Hall he talked to Mr. Hobson himself, he did, got me a position: I board in winters with him and I run all his errands, cut his wood, stoke his fires, I even do some cooking."

"Well, well, so you're learning a lot, I suppose."

"I am. I work all winter for Mr. Hobson, and he lets me come to school, and I work all summer for Mr. Hall. I'm helping with accounts and stuff because Mr. Hobson learned me them figures 'n things like 'at."

"Taught me, Ben," James corrected.

"Oh yeah, I always forget that one. Makes him crazy. Well, I'd best be going or he'll think I'm a lazy rascal — that's what he calls me sometimes."

Catherine smiled. "Well, come and see us, Ben. Make sure you do."

"I will that, ma'am." He hoisted his bag of flour, almost bigger than he was, and steadying it with his one good arm, off he went up the hill.

James wondered if they shouldn't go directly to the Garretts' home. But he decided they should first learn about the commission, and head for the municipal courtroom where the commission was meeting.

He and Catherine traded looks. He could see that she was nervous about being back in her hometown after a three-year absence. How the time had flown! The last visit had been the spring of that terrible famine, the "year of no summer" in fact.

Once at the courthouse, James saw quite a few faces of old friends, some from Paspébiac. But no sign of M. Blanquart. He spotted the McRaes from down Hopetown way and, of course, John Ross.

And who should be there but Catherine's brothers, John and Joseph. At least they would have no trouble: their land had been given them by grant from the King. But they also occupied other waste land they had cleared behind the village. They would be wanting title to that, too. Unless all of it were seized by some greedy bureaucrat from Montreal and Quebec.

James greeted John, shook his hand and, after more pleasantries, asked, "You got out of debtors prison all right I heard."

"Back then? Oh yes, we only spent a week. Big mistake. We soon rectified it, once Father arranged to get us out."

"And are your parents at home?"

"They are." James could see in John's face that he was worried about what lay ahead. "I reckon they must be expecting a visit from yez. Half the country's gathering in New Carlisle now, for this here land commission."

"Have they mentioned anything?"

"No. We don't talk about you fellas around the house. Only when me and Joseph are alone. We've been wondering how you was both making out."

"Catherine," James said, "wait here with your brothers and see what you can find out. I'll go face your mother and father." He said it with such resolution that Catherine was ready to obey. She dropped her eyes.

"We'll be waiting here for the result." Joseph shook his hand warmly.

With resolution, but also trepidation, James went off and soon came knocking at the Garretts'. He heard movement inside, and William Senior opened the door.

Mr. Garrett looked as if struck by a giant fly swatter. He paused for a second and then turned and called inside, "Eleanor. There's someone here to see you." He opened the door courteously and then limped across to his favourite chair, and wordlessly sat down.

Eleanor came downstairs and stopped. "James!" She hurried across to give him a hug and a kiss. "We've been waiting so long for you to come." She turned to her husband. "Haven't we, William?"

William looked up and met her eyes. Then he dropped his. "I reckon we have." He busied himself getting out his pipe and his tobacco.

"Well, come and sit down. Let me make you a cup of tea. I must hear all the news."

"Thank you, Mrs. Garrett."

"I thought we agreed you'd call me mother," Eleanor said. She busied herself getting the kettle ready for tea, not meeting his eyes. "We've heard the sad news about you losing your own parent while she was en route to live with you. We were very sorry to hear that, James. So now, you really must look on me as your mother instead."

He looked at her. Such a warm feeling. Yes, he would find that easy, given time. "Very well, 'Mother.' And you know, I have a surprise for you."

William looked up from his pipe. Eleanor turned nervously.

"Your very own grandchildren, and your daughter, are waiting at the courthouse, where the land commission is meeting. They dearly wish to be received here in your home, as I have been. Perhaps, then, we might even stay with you a few days."

Eleanor straightened. "Those are the words we've waited to hear for three long years." She turned again and looked at William. "Haven't we, William?"

"I suppose so."

Eleanor put her hands on her hips, angrily.

William glanced up, and then obviously had a change of heart. "Aye, that we have." He proceeded to struggle out of his chair. "It's been far too long, that it has. What's done is done. And a man can always turn over a new leaf, that's what I always say." He glanced at Eleanor who turned away, exasperated at his gall. William then stumped across to James and held out a freckled hand.

James looked in his eyes. He saw the eyes of an old man, weary and contrite. James gripped his hand and put another on his father-in-law's shoulder. "No man can say how happy this makes me."

"Tea'll be ready in a few minutes," Eleanor said.

"To hell with tea! Let's get right out that door, luv, and run up to the courthouse and find our daughter." William motioned. "We'd best not waste another minute."

It seemed to James, as he hurried along with the older

couple, that the whole thing had taken place so easily. No great dramatic scene, no thundering denunciations, no fierce anger and shaking of fists. Well, why not? It was as it should be. Lonely souls, getting back together.

If only the land commission battle could be this successfully won.

As they rounded the corner, James saw Catherine turn and gasp. Her hands went to her face. Could it be true, she must be thinking. And yes, he said to himself, only too true. Why didn't we do this last year?

Catherine broke into a run to meet her mother as they wrapped each other in their arms, crying and laughing as only a mother and daughter can.

Then Catherine disengaged herself and came over to throw her arms around her father, and kiss him, too.

From the look on his face, William Sr. seemed mightily satisfied. "Now, where are our two grandchildren?"

James could not help but notice the firmness in his voice as he pronounced both words: "two grandchildren." So John had been accepted at last.

Eleanor bent down and hugged little Mariah while William Sr. picked up little John. For a few moments the little boy looked frightened, but then seeing the joy in the old man's face, he soon relaxed and laughed delightedly as William hoisted him up in the air.

James noticed that Joseph had been watching from afar, and he now came over. "Together again," was all he said, but his eyes brimmed with tears. "John's inside. He'll be out in the second."

Before he had finished speaking, John came out through the doors, saw them, and hurried across to the happy family.

"You'll never believe it! All you have to do is go in, and make your petition with one witness. And the land is yours!"

"You mean, it's a commission to give us a deed to our land, free and clear?" Such good news! After all those worries. But so much better to worry beforehand and find the truth agreeable, than the other way around. He looked at his wife. They had weathered so much together: the building of the farmhouse, the year of no summer, the accepting of the two children, on and on.

"We have our land," she beamed, "and we have our family. What could be better?"

"Nothing in the whole world, my dearest," James said. "Our land and our family indeed."

Author's Note

My great grandfather fought in 1805 under Admiral Nelson in the Battle of Trafalgar. When his man o'war, the Bellerophon, *came to the New World, he jumped ship and built his new home in the Gaspé. His youngest son, my grandfather James, was born in 1835, and my father, Eric, also a youngest son, was born in 1893.*

To commemorate these three ancestors, I write this series of largely fictional accounts of a family that helped found a real English community on the shores of the Gaspé Coast, and lived and farmed there for two centuries.

ACKNOWLEDGEMENTS

I would like to acknowledge with real gratitude the many who have helped me write this novel, and apologize to those who have also provided insights but may not be mentioned herein.

As before, Roger Pelletier, former Director of the Micmac Interpretation Centre in Gaspé, continued to provide me with great help.

Prof. Danielle Cyr of York University, foremost expert on the Micmac language, summers on the Coast and has co-authored a splendid Micmac dictionary. She helped me with words and concepts, and, finally, read the completed manuscript, adding valuable changes.

My cousin Elton Hayes, horse-breeder par excellence and one of the many custodians of Shigawake's oral tradition, provided me with a living source of animal husbandry, and much of the local history. Raymond Garrett, a Pabos schoolteacher, has laboured over the years to provide a comprehensive genealogy of the Garretts and Almonds. He didn't mind, in this work of fiction, the odd discrepancy in dates. In oral tradition, our family has some Micmac blood. I have presumed Catherine claimed John as her son and, to protect him, chose another date for his birth and baptism. (John shows up in genealogies as being born after Mariah.)

Carl and Lois Hayes, intrepid birders and the unquestioned historians of Shigawake families, helped me enormously with the arrival and lineage of our first settlers here in Shigawake.

David Cordingly's impressive, readable, and at the same time scholarly volume *The Billy Ruffian* (nickname of the *Bellerophon*) came along at just the right moment.

In New Richmond, Joan Dow, who founded the British Heritage Village and its fine genealogy department, was of great help in looking up our mutual antecedents.

I must mention and thank two other friendly cardiologists: Doctors Suhail Dohad and Ronald Karlsberg, who have kept me on my feet, and Cynthia Patterson, who challenges me to run faster, just to keep up with her. I should thank my former housekeeper for providing me with material from which to shape one of the characters herein. And finally, a most important thank you to my sharp-eyed friend David Stansfield, himself a fine novelist, who helped with my website and also added many finishing touches to this book.

I am blessed also with marvellous advisor-readers. Nicholas Etheridge, a former diplomat of no mean intelligence and scholarly wisdom, has pointed out some discrepancies and anachronisms. Rex King, a novelist herself, has been a continual source of encouragement, perceptive editing, and support. Diana Colman, a good friend from Oxford fifty years ago and herself a novelist and grandparent, gave me wonderful suggestions. Peter Duffell, a distinguished British film director, who wrote novels in his Keble College digs when the rest of us at Oxford were just learning to spell (well, perhaps a bit more) did read this thoroughly and gave structural and helpful hints. The Rev. Susan Kline has been a great inspiration and gave many good notes, as did the playwright <u>Oren Safdie</u>, whom I have known since he wore knee-pants in Montreal on his daddy Moshe's lap.

Finally, my cousin <u>Ted Wright</u> thankfully solved many of the smaller (and larger) problems during our discussions while fighting the pernicious advance of Queen Anne's Lace into our beetroot. After a good farm breakfast together around five-thirty, he would sally forth to make crab traps for the leading trap-maker in the Maritimes, Camille Gignac. Ted's unparalleled store of knowledge of history (and almost everything else) in science, crafts, and local lore, intersected so often with the interests of this book.

APPENDIX: HISTORICAL BACKGROUND

May 1816 — First Historical Document: James Required as Witness

George the Third by the grace of God of the United Kingdom of Great Britain and Ireland, King, Defender of the Faith,

To James Oldman [sic] alias Thomas Manning of Hopetown, farmer and fisherman, and

John Rafter of Cox Township, fishermen and maritimer

You are hereby required to be and appear before our Judge of our Provincial Court for the said Inferior district of Gaspe at the Court House of Bonaventure on Monday the twenty-seventh day of May instant at 10 of the clock in the forenoon, to testify in truth and give evidence in that cause now pending and undetermined between:

Jacobson Belair of Cox township, plaintiff, and

William Garrett of Cox township, Junior, defendant

as to slander of the defendant against the plaintiff as heresay

Hereof fail not on pain of law

Witness the Honourable William Crawford, our judge of our said Provincial Court, the twenty-fifth day of May in the year of our Lord one thousand eight hundred and sixteen and in the fifty-sixth year of our reign.

Amasa BeeBe, Clark of Court.

December 1816 — Second Historical Document (Excerpt): James's Petition for Food

That your petitioner… Was led to the sea service from 15 years old and served his Majesty the King… as a seaman in the fleet under Lord Keith at the taking of Alexandria in Egypt, being then in the Bellerophon Man of War, [under]

Captain Pratt, and has been settled in the Bay of Chaleur for five years having then married the daughter of William Garrett Snr in Cox Township.

...has occupied a piece of waste land in East Nouvelle aforesaid where he lives with his wife and two children, and that last spring he planted two barrels and half potatoes but from the frosts in August has had a very bad crop, not more than eight barrels and had no other. ...That your petitioner had an infirmity in his back by a strain in lifting of barrel of potatoes into Amos Hall's cart but that he is now pretty well recovered from that complaint.

December 1819 — Third Historical Document: Grant of Land to James

Claim by James Almond of Hopetown, farmer, for lot #40 in Hope aforesaid containing 200 acres on a front of 5 acres, bounded on the west by lot #39, on the East by the Shigawake brook, which divides it from #1 Port Daniel, in front by the Bay de Chaleurs and in rear by waste lands of the Crown Division on lateral lines No. 5 West magnetically ~ occupancy for six years last past.
Witness examined 29 July 1820: James A. Nielsen
published in both languages in the Quebec Gazette in 1823.

November 1817 — Reference to John and William Junior, Debtors Prison

On Nov 6th, 1817 the Garrett brothers William Jr and John built and registered the schooner LARK (official number 9017137) in Quebec City. The Lark may have arrived in Quebec on Aug 10, 1817 with a cargo of fish and oil. The prison records for Quebec City have a William Garrett Jr and a John Garrett in prison for debt (for the sails and other ship parts?) and unpaid bills in November 1817. Subsequently released Nov 10th by order of Philippe Aubert de Gaspé, Esqre. Sheriff.
Raymond Garrett, genealogist.
Source: Centre d'archives de Québec, E17 (1960-01-036/1569-1578)
Registre de la prison de Québec: 1813–1823, vol. 1, f. 81 Numero: 740

The Year of No Summer, 1816

In 1815 on the island of Sumbawa in Indonesia, a handsome and long-quiescent mountain named Tambora exploded spectacularly, killing a hundred thousand people with its blast and associated tsunamis.

It was the biggest volcanic explosion in ten thousand years — 150 times the size of Mount St. Helens, equivalent to sixty thousand Hiroshima-sized atom bombs. Thirty-six cubic miles of smoky ash, dust and grit had diffused through the atmosphere, obscuring the sun's rays and causing the earth to cool.
Source: Bill Bryson, *A Short History of Nearly Everything* (Toronto: Anchor Canada, 2004)

There is a time lag between a volcanic eruption and a change in weather patterns caused by the length of time needed for stratospheric winds to distribute the volcanic dust particles around the world.

Between May and September 1816, southern Quebec was affected by a series of cold waves that killed crops and led to near famine conditions in some parts. During one such cold spell between June 6th and 10th, 30–36cms snow lay on the ground in Quebec City. Meanwhile on June 6th and 8th it snowed in Montreal (Neil Davids, 1976). Sub-zero temperatures during June blackened crops and froze ponds, killing wildfowl. Some mornings in July and August were decidedly chilly and probably frosty, whilst hard frosts on 11th, 12th and 27th September ended the already shortened growing season.
Source: Dan Suri, www.dandantheweatherman.com

Report on Typhus in the Year of No Summer, 1816

Weather in Europe and other regions of the globe was abnormal in 1816. In Europe, the cold and wet weather contributed to a disastrous harvest as crops rotted in the field. Famine, food riots, grain hoarding, and government embargoes resulted. These cold, moist weather patterns may have contributed to the typhus epidemic of 1816–1819 in Europe that killed approximately 200,000 people, and the cholera outbreak of 1816–1817 which originated in Bengal and spread throughout the world.
Source: The Verner E. Suomi Virtual Museum

Paul Almond is one of Canada's pre-eminent film and television directors, and he has directed and produced over 130 television dramas for the CBC, BBC, ABC and Granada Television. Paul Almond lives on the Gaspé Peninsula in Quebec and Malibu, California. For a reading group guide, further historical background and more, visit him online at www.thealfordsaga.com